Orphan Wish Island

Sarah Anne Carter

Orphan Wish Island

Histria Kids

Las Vegas ◊ Chicago ◊ Palm Beach

Published in the United States of America by
Histria Books, a division of Histria LLC
7181 N. Hualapai Way, Ste. 130-86
Las Vegas, NV 89166 USA
HistriaBooks.com

Histria Kids is an imprint of Histria Books. Titles published under the imprints of Histria Books are distributed worldwide.

Library of Congress Control Number: 2020949877

ISBN 978-1-59211-085-8 (hardcover)
ISBN 978-1-59211-147-3 (softbound)
ISBN 978-1-59211-221-0 (eBook)

Contents

Dedication

This book is dedicated to all the young people who live their lives missing someone they love.

Chapter 1

Miriam closed her book and sighed. Another birthday was almost over. Her finger was holding her place. She was at the end of a chapter, and her eyes were feeling heavy. The window seat in her bedroom was one of the few good things about living with her grandmother. She read there every night until she got tired. She had to be almost exhausted to fall asleep here. The house creaked and groaned, and she wasn't used to all the noises.

She looked around her legs for her bookmark. The last birthday card her parents had given her when she was eight had a cat bookmark attached to the card. She used it in each and every book she read. Every time she started or finished reading, she thought of them and wondered what they would say if they were here.

The bookmark was tucked next to the window. Miriam grabbed it and then saw the streetlamps flicker, which caught her eye because they flickered three times in quick succession. She blinked and then rubbed her eyes. The lamp on her dresser hadn't flickered, so it probably wasn't a power outage. Then the streetlamp did it again. She could see everything clearly outside in the light of the full moon. It was so bright; the moon cast shadows off the tombstones in the cemetery across the street. The lights flickered a third time, and then the power went out completely — both on the street and in the house.

Miriam swung her legs down to the floor, put the bookmark in her book, and put the book down on the faded maroon pillow that served as a cushion to the window seat. Even with no lights on, she could see everything in her room clearly because of the moonlight. It was as if the moon's rays were shining directly into her room.

Then Miriam noticed a glow coming from across the room around the attic door. She had explored in there the first week she was at Grandma's and only found a few old boxes of memorabilia. She wanted to look through it someday for family history's sake; however, nothing in there seemed fascinating enough to put up with the amount of dust in the small space. Grandma kept her important papers, photos, and holiday decorations in tubs in the basement.

As she approached the door, she realized that the door itself had a glow. There were shining words on the door ...

> On a full moon, when the lights blink three,
>
> the door will connect to your family tree.
>
> Only orphans may enter and find what they seek,
>
> Open the door. Be brave, not meek.

She ran her finger over the words. They weren't carved into the door but seemed to be written on the door with the moon's light. The light of the words showed on her hand if she put it on them. She was more curious than scared. She wondered if she was dreaming. If it was a dream, she should just go through the door and see what happened. It couldn't be real ...

She opened the door and had to cover her eyes and squint against the glare as she walked through. She stepped onto white sand and saw a few palm trees and the ocean off in the distance under a clear blue sky. It was beautiful. There were five other children near one of the palm trees. She decided to go talk to them and see where she was. As she took another step, the door to the attic closed behind her. After hearing it close, she turned back and saw its outline in the air with her name written across it. Seeing that, she knew she could get back.

Miriam walked over to the other children. The breeze made it the perfect temperature as it gently moved her straight brown hair. The smell of the ocean surrounded her. The other five children stopped talking to each other and turned toward Miriam, waiting for her to approach. She waved shyly, and two of the girls waved back. As she got closer, she could see there were four girls and one boy. The boy had black hair and was leaning against a palm tree. The girls all looked about her age. Miriam was just a few steps away from the closest girl, who had short red hair. Miriam was about to introduce herself to the group when they were all surrounded by creatures that Miriam could at first only describe as fairies — but human-sized fairies.

"Are these all?" one asked as she hovered behind the boy, who had stopped leaning against the tree and turned to stare at the creature.

"There were at least triple this amount last year — and that had been the smallest year," another one spoke.

"Guess most of us can go back home if that's all there is," another spoke. "Stella, Luna, and Metea, can you cover these few?"

"Yes, Zara," said the one behind the boy. Miriam had been staring at her, too. She had pale yellow wings and wore a matching dress that had sparkles all over it. Her hair was dark brown and curly. She stopped flying and landed next to the boy.

Two other creatures landed, one right beside Miriam.

"My name is Luna," one said to the group. Her dress was navy blue, but her wings were white. Her hair was also curly, but blonde. The creatures that hadn't landed then took off to the sky. All the children watched them fly away until they couldn't see them anymore and then turned to the three on the ground.

"I'm Stella," said the one in yellow.

"And, I'm Metea," said the last one, who wore a lilac dress and dark purple wings. Her hair was pink and in a pixie cut.

"What is this place, and what are you guys?" the boy asked. "I really do think I'm dreaming."

All of the children, including Miriam, nodded their heads in agreement. It must be a dream, Miriam thought — a crazy, fun one.

"You are on Orphan Wish Island, OWI for short. We are Volturians. We live here and among you. There is much to your world that you don't see. Your parents may have left your lives physically, but they were given the ability to help you on your life's path by giving you access to this island and a wish granted each year," Stella explained.

"Wishes?" one of the girls said. The girl was tall and skinny and wore a basketball t-shirt. "Like birthday candles and throwing pennies into fountains? That stuff never works."

"Of course it doesn't work," Metea said. "You humans can't make magic work in your world, Amelia. It's probably a good thing, too."

"Hey, how do you know my name?" the girl in the basketball t-shirt asked. Apparently, her name was Amelia.

"Your parents told us all about you," Stella said. "Parents who leave children behind as orphans are allowed to stop here before they move on and leave six wishes for their children. It might be easier if I show you. Please follow me."

Stella led the way on foot while Metea and Luna flew ahead of the group to a tree about 30 feet away. It was the same height as the palm trees scattered about the island, but its leaves were star-shaped and a shiny green color — when the light caught on a leaf, it shone like metal. As they got closer, Miriam could see there was also a pale yellow fruit or type of nut on the tree, shaped like a star.

"This, children, is the Wishing Tree," Stella said. "If you look closely, you will find a Starfruit with your name on it. When you pick it, you will hear a message from your parents. Only you will be able to hear it. To initiate your wishes, you must eat the fruit. Your parents have been granted one wish for you each year for the next six years, and you may also make your own wish each year, too. When you are 18, you may come back here one more time to hear a final message from your parents and send them one back."

The kids all looked at each other. Miriam had a hard time believing it was real. If this were just a dream, her grandma would love it. It wouldn't hurt to at least eat the fruit and see what happened.

"Is this for real?" the boy said. "It sounds a bit crazy."

Miriam and one of the girls — the one with straight, blond hair down to her waist — took a few steps toward the tree. Miriam looked at the Starfruit more closely and saw her name on one just a little above her head to the left.

"This one does have my name on it!" She reached up to grab it as the rest of the kids started looking closer at the tree and its fruit.

"Hey — there's my name!"

The fairies hung back, letting the children discover and believe on their own. They always guessed amongst themselves who would take the first bite. None of them had guessed Miriam, so they were all surprised when they saw her take a few steps away from the tree with the Starfruit and take a bite. It tasted sweet — like sparkling strawberry lemonade. Miriam had just barely swallowed her first bite when she heard a familiar voice.

"Oh, Miriam, we love you so much!" Miriam heard her mother say, just like she did every night when she was alive. Miriam looked all around and up but didn't see her mother anywhere.

"We miss you so much!" she then heard her father say. She sat down, closed her eyes, and started crying softly as she listened. She didn't notice that the other children were starting to grab their own Starfruit and take bites, too. She just listened.

"We are so glad you decided to come to this island," her mother said. "We know it can't be easy without us there to help you grow up, but we made wishes that we hope will help you as you become an adult."

"We can't tell you what we wished for until you turn 18. They're all good, though!" her dad said. "We hope you make good wishes, too."

"It's so hard ..." Miriam started. Her mother interrupted her.

"We can't be there to see you. We had to make these wishes before heading on. This is a recorded message."

"But," her dad continued, "they said if you make your wish each year, we can talk to you when you come back at 18. I can't wait to see what a beautiful young lady you turn into!"

"We love you more than the world! Be good and be kind," her mom said.

"And be smart, Miribug," her dad said. "Bye."

Miriam hugged her knees tighter and whispered, "Bye." She loved hearing her parents' voice again, but it made her miss them as much as she did right after they died. They said the same thing they told her every time they'd said goodbye when they were alive. She went over the conversation in her head a few times before she finally looked up and remembered where she was.

The other kids were all holding their bitten Starfruit and closing their eyes. One by one, they all opened their eyes and walked back to where Stella, Luna, and Metea were standing. Even though Miriam was the first to finish hearing from her parents, she was the last to go stand by the fairies. She had begun thinking about what she should wish.

"Children," Metea said, "we know it's hard to hear from your parents." She walked over and put her arm around Amelia. "Some of you lost your parents just recently, and others have been without their parents for years."

"When you are ready to make your wish for this year, you need to take another bite of your Starfruit, then say your wish out loud," Luna told them. "You will then need to pick a spot to plant your Starfruit. A tree will grow with enough Starfruit for the rest of your wishes. Each year on this date, your door will glow, allowing you to come back to this island and make your wish. If you come back every year, you will be able to talk to your parents when you turn 18, and they will reveal what they wished for you each year."

"You can take your time here as well," Stella said. "Time does not pass on Earth while you are here, although you may get tired and hungry if you stay too long. There was once a boy who tried to stay as long as he could, but after two days, I whispered, 'Cheeseburger,' to him, and he finally went home." All the fairies chuckled at the story.

"What do you eat if there's no food here?" the boy said.

"We don't need to eat, Aaron," Luna said. "It's kind of like magic here, but better."

"Do you have any recommendations on wishes?" the girl with short, red hair asked.

"We can't give you specific ideas, Lexi," Stella said. "In general, though, you should wish for something that can help you be a better person. Maybe try wishing what you think your parents would wish for you."

"Oh, we didn't tell them what they couldn't wish for yet!" Metea said loudly. She grabbed the shortest girl's arm quickly to stop her from taking a bite. "Elaine, wait just a minute!

"You cannot wish for money, cars, a new house, a change in your appearance, or people coming back from the dead. You can wish for a small change in your life that is under your control. You can ask to be nicer, more organized, or a better test taker, but you can't ask for better grades without the work."

"Can I ask to be the lead in the school musical?" Miriam asked. She had really enjoyed being on stage at the various school music performances, and in sixth grade, there was a musical she could try out for as an option for music class. It sounded more exciting than choir or music theory.

"Yes, you can, as long as you are willing to work on memorizing your lines," Luna said. "It's a wish that will make your life better, but it's not a completely magical wish. We help you make your life a little bit better since your parents aren't there to help you."

"So, I can wish to make the basketball team and be one of the better players as long as I still practice?" Amelia asked.

"Yes, exactly," Metea said.

"Well, that will be my wish then," Amelia said. She then took a bite of her Starfruit and said, "I wish to be a star basketball player at school this year."

"Great wish," Luna said. "Let me help you plant that Starfruit." Luna took Amelia about 20 feet away from the group and helped her dig a small hole and plant the Starfruit. Then, she walked her to her door. Amelia opened her door and turned to wave at the group. "See you next year!"

Miriam was about to make her wish about the school musical when Aaron spoke up, wishing to do better at school. She then heard Lexi wish about having more friends. That's a good one, Miriam thought — maybe she'd wish for that next year. Being in the school musical may solve her friend issue anyway, she thought.

"I wish to get a main part in the school musical," Miriam said after taking a bite of the Starfruit. Luna came to her and helped her, just like she'd helped Amelia.

"Do most people come back every year?" Miriam asked Luna as they walked to her door.

"Sadly, no," she said. "Less than half make it to 18, but I have a feeling you will be here when you're 18. I can see you loved your parents very much and that they loved you."

"I miss them. I don't think that will ever go away."

Luna stopped in front of Miriam's door. "Enjoy the musical. See you next year!"

And just like that, Miriam was back in her bedroom. She opened the attic door back up quickly, but all she saw was the dark space with boxes everywhere.

"I need to go to sleep," she said to herself. "I bet I just imagined all that."

She changed into her pajamas, brushed her teeth, and washed her face. Then, she went to tell her grandmother that she was going to bed, but she was already asleep in her recliner chair. Miriam went and plopped into her bed. She knew sleep would come soon as she was really tired. The conversation with her parents kept playing over and over in her head, and they were the first things she thought of when she woke up in the morning.

Chapter 2

Miriam's parents had been dead for four years and three days. Since they died in a car accident two days before her birthday, she always knew how long they had been gone.

Her grandmother had baked her a cake from a box mix with icing from a tub for her 12th birthday, but she could barely force herself to eat two bites of it. She politely thanked her grandmother for the cake and the bookstore gift card and then said she was tired and wanted to go to bed early. What she really wanted to say was that she hated birthday cake. Someone had thought it would be a good idea to have a birthday cake for her at her parents' funeral. It had been a small, round cake with "Happy 8th Birthday, Miriam" written in pink — her least favorite color. Just having pink on her cake was a reminder that the two people who knew her best were gone. She grabbed the cake when no one was looking and tossed it into the trashcan at the funeral home. Then, she asked her aunt if they could leave.

She had been staying with her Aunt Suzy and Uncle Mike on the night of the car accident. It was a Friday night, and her parents were going to a musical in downtown Kansas City. Her dad was reluctant to go, but her mom had repeatedly told him that he would enjoy the storyline. Her mom loved going to the theater but didn't get to go very often. She had won the tickets in a raffle to raise money to renovate the staff lounge at the hospital where she worked as a nurse. Her mom and Aunt Suzy were both nurses. They were only two years apart, with her mom being the oldest, and they had even gone to the same college for a while. She ate pizza with her aunt and uncle, and then she watched a movie with Aunt Suzy before heading to bed in their guest room. Her aunt woke her up early the next morning, and Miriam knew something was wrong right away. Aunt Suzy's face was all red, and she was crying.

"Miriam, I'm so sorry, but your parents... there was a bad accident on their way home... they didn't make it."

"What? No! Where are they? Are they at the hospital?" Miriam jumped out of bed and started heading toward the front door. She needed to go wherever her parents were right then. Uncle Mike gently stopped her before she opened the front door. He hugged her, and she started crying. He walked her to the couch in the living room, and Aunt Suzy sat down beside her. They all cried for a long time.

The day after her parents didn't come home, her aunt and uncle took her by her house to get some of her things, and they said she could stay with them for as long as it took to get things settled. She didn't have any other aunts or uncles. Her grandparents on her mom's side lived across town, and her other grandparents lived in an assisted living facility in Phoenix. Even though Aunt Suzy and Uncle Mike have been married for six years, they didn't have any children. Miriam was in their wedding as their flower girl, and she got to spend a lot of time with them. They always showed up at her school performances.

Her grandparents were over at her house Saturday afternoon, too, to help work on the funeral planning. Miriam stayed in the guest room until dinnertime, not wanting to hear them talking about burying her parents. She laid down in bed, trying to read, but really trying harder to think about nothing.

Her grandmother knocked on the door and came in.

"We're going to eat dinner soon, Miriam. Mind if I come in?" She sat down on the bed and patted beside her — the cue for Miriam to come sit by her. Miriam sat up and moved to sit by her grandma, who then put her arm around her.

"I wanted to let you know that the funeral will be Tuesday morning. We'll go over the details with you on Monday. But we wanted to ask you if you wanted to do anything for your birthday tomorrow? We know you probably aren't in the mood to celebrate, but we could go to your favorite restaurant, or I could make you a cake ..."

"Oh, Grandma," was all Miriam could say before she started crying again. Grandma held her for a while, then told her she could think about it and let them know later. She pulled out a tissue from her pocket and gave it to Miriam.

"Let's get you some food, dear." Even though she wasn't very hungry, Miriam followed her grandmother out of the room.

She ended up spending most of her eighth birthday in her new room — her aunt and uncle's guest room — reading. Her aunt or grandma came to check on her every couple of hours. They tried to be upbeat and not mention anything about her parents that day, but Miriam kept wishing over and over that they would be the ones who would walk through the door when she heard a knock. She had told her grandma that morning that she really didn't want to celebrate her birthday at all. However, they had ordered pizza from her favorite place for dinner with all the toppings she loved — pepperoni, chicken, green peppers, and bacon. Grandma had made chocolate chip cookies, too, which were another one of her favorite things. She knew they were celebrating, even though they were trying not to. At least there were no presents.

Before going up to bed, she hugged everyone and thanked them. Her grandpa hugged her extra tight and whispered a very quiet, "Happy birthday, Miribug," in her ear. She smiled at that and hugged him tight back.

When she opened the door to her room, she saw a present on her bed. She could tell from across the room that it was her mother's handwriting on the card. She froze at the door then felt a hand on her shoulder.

"I found this on your parents' dresser when we went to your house. I think they would want you to have it today, but it's up to you when you want to open it," Aunt Suzy said. Miriam looked up at her aunt and could see she was nervous. She was fiddling with the cross necklace she always wore.

"Thank you," Miriam said. She started crying again, and her aunt hugged her.

"You are loved, Miriam. They loved you very much, and we love you, too."

Miriam nodded then moved to go into the bedroom. Her aunt started walking down the stairs, and Miriam shut her door.

Part of her didn't want to open the present because once she did, it would be over, and she wouldn't be getting anything else from her parents ever. She always loved getting presents, though and wondered what they had gotten her this year. She decided to open the present but save the card for later when she needed to "hear" from them. The present was a beautifully illustrated hardback book of Robin Hood. It was her parents' favorite story, and they read it to her every year at bedtime around her birthday month once the weather started getting colder. They usually finished the book before Valentine's Day. There was writing from both her parents inside the cover, but she couldn't read it through her tears. She was remembering how last year, when they finished reading the book, a few pages had fallen out of the paperback copy.

"It's time to get a new book," Miriam had told her mother.

"We can tape these pages back in," her mother replied.

"We could, or we could just get a new copy. I know! You could keep that one and buy a new one for me. I'll need my own copy when I go to college anyway," Miriam said.

"Very true. This book is one your father gave me when we were dating. You should have your own copy," her mother said before tucking her in and kissing her forehead. "Sleep well, Miribug."

Miriam ended up living with her aunt and uncle until the summer before she turned 12, when they left to go be missionaries in Kenya. They had been thinking of going before her parents died since they weren't going to be able to have any children of their own. They were going to work in an orphanage and be house parents to a dozen children. They had put off going so Miriam could adjust to her new life, but after four years, they told her they felt the call to go. She moved in with her grandma. She was happy about it because she loved her grandma and knew she was lonely after Grandpa died last year from a heart attack in his sleep. She wondered how many other 11-year-olds had been to three funerals in their lifetimes. The worst part about moving to Grandma's house was that it was on the other side of Kansas City, in Missouri instead of Kansas, which meant changing schools. She had exactly one "friend" at the new school, and that was the girl who lived next door, Stephanie Risner. Stephanie and Miriam had nothing in common except their age, location, and school. She met Stephanie three years ago when her family was moving into the house. Miriam had spent the weekend with her grandparents so her aunt and uncle could go celebrate their anniversary in Omaha. It was a drizzly fall Saturday, so Miriam put on her rain boots and raincoat before heading out to meet the girl she saw getting out of the minivan before the moving truck showed up. She rang the doorbell, and the new girl came to the door.

"Hi! I'm Miriam. My grandparents live next door. Welcome to the neighborhood!"

"Are those pink hearts on your rain boots? Ick! Pink is so childish."

Miriam didn't know what to say back. She was stunned by the girl's attitude.

"Well, I guess there's all kinds of tastes. Do you live next door?" the girl asked.

"No, but I visit a lot. I live across town on the Kansas side."

"We used to live in a nice apartment in downtown Kansas City, but my parents want more room since I'll be a big sister in a few months. How old are you?"

"I'm nine. You?" Miriam asked.

"I'm nine, too. When's your birthday? Mine is August 23."

"Mine is October 17."

"I'm older!"

"Stephanie? Who's at the door?" a woman's voice called from in the house.

"Just a neighbor girl," Stephanie shouted back. "I better go. My mom is close to being on bed rest, and I have to help take care of her and unpack."

Stephanie went back into the house and closed the door. Miriam said bye and slowly walked back home. She had never met anyone who acted like Stephanie. Maybe that's what city girls acted like. Her parents had met in college in downtown Chicago, though, and they didn't act like that after living in the city. She wished she could tell her mom about Stephanie. She'd have to write in her diary about it tonight. She'd written about her day almost every day after her parents' funeral. She pretended she was writing them letters like they were just away on a trip. She just wished she could hear back from them.

Chapter 3

Miriam woke up and looked around her room. *The island couldn't have been real last night*, she thought; *it must have been a dream*. But then, she closed her eyes and replayed the message her parents had sent her — in the dream. She had to tell her grandma all about it. Grandma asked her every morning if she had dreamt the night before and always listened intently if she had a dream to share.

She threw back the faded flower comforter that used to be her mother's and got out of bed. She glanced at the attic door and decided to check once more to see what was behind it. She opened it and saw nothing but boxes. As she was shutting the door, something shiny caught her eye on the ground by her foot. She bent down and picked it up — it was a Starfruit seed! She had seen them when she planted her Starfruit — they were a shiny pale yellow and were shaped like stars. She knew she hadn't brought one back on purpose, but maybe one had stuck to her clothing.

"Or, maybe the fairies put it there to show us that it was real..." Miriam whispered to herself as she stared at the seed in her palm. "What if it was real ...?"

Miriam sat back down on her bed and replayed the words from her parents in her head again. She grabbed her journal and wrote it all down — word for word. She started describing the island and the fruit and the rules about the wishes. She was almost done when she heard her grandmother call her name.

"Miriam! Are you up? I thought I heard you. The bus comes in 15 minutes, and you still haven't eaten. Your eggs and toast are getting cold."

Miriam had totally forgotten it was a school day.

"I'm coming, Grandma!"

She put her journal back under her mattress, put the seed in her jewelry box, and threw on a pair of jeans and a long-sleeved T-shirt. She brushed her teeth and hair and was downstairs less than five minutes after her grandmother called for her.

Every morning, whether it was a school day or not, her grandmother had breakfast ready for her by 7:30 a.m. The bus came at 7:55 a.m. On the weekends, she sometimes made muffins or pancakes, but it was always scrambled eggs, buttered toast, and orange juice during the week. While she was getting tired of having the same thing every morning, Miriam was glad that she didn't have to get her own breakfast ready, so she didn't complain. Her parents had helped her prepare breakfast each morning before they died, but when she lived with her aunt and uncle, she was on her own to grab some cereal, a granola bar, or fruit. Orange juice was a treat with her aunt and uncle, and it was one of her favorite things to have at breakfast.

Grandma also made her a lunch, and like breakfast, it was often the same thing over and over, but she had also had to make her lunch at her aunt and uncle's house or buy school lunch. She most often got the school lunch, but there were very few hot lunches that she actually liked. If she asked Grandma if she could buy lunch when there was spaghetti or tacos on the menu, she gave Miriam money to take with her. Most days, though, she got a sandwich on homemade bread, an apple, some carrots, and a homemade cookie. She had asked her grandmother if she could have a soda to take in for lunch when school started. While Grandma said that stuff wasn't good for anyone, she also agreed that at almost 12, Miriam could start making her own decisions.

"Sorry I was down late this morning, Grandma," Miriam said as she sat down to eat. She had less than ten minutes to get out to the curb. "I had the most interesting dream — it seemed so real."

"What was it about?"

"It was an island with fairies, and I could make a wish," Miriam said, then finished her last bite of toast and her orange juice. She looked at the clock. "I'll have to tell you more later, but I wished I could get a lead part in the school musical this year."

"That would be fun if it happened. Did the island have a name?" Grandma asked as she took Miriam's sack lunch and soda from the refrigerator and handed it to her. Miriam put her dishes in the sink and grabbed her lunch and soda to put in her backpack by the door.

"Orphan Wish Island," Miriam said as she put on her shoes, dark purple fleece coat, and backpack.

Her grandmother put her hand on Miriam's arm as she reached to open the front door.

"Orphan Wish Island? Are you sure it was a dream?"

"What do you mean?" Miriam didn't want her grandma to know Miriam thought it was real.

"I've been there." They stared at each other for a few seconds, and then they heard the bus pull up in front of the house. Miriam pulled the door open and ran outside so the bus driver would see her and not leave without her.

"We'll talk after school, Miriam," Grandma promised. "Be good! I love you!"

Miriam got on the bus and sat in her assigned seat — six rows back by the window on the left. She could see Grandma wave to her from the window, and she waved back. If her grandma had been to the island, then it must be real! She had really heard a message from her parents. They'd actually made a wish for her that would come true every year, and she got to make a wish of her own every year. She would have a lead role in the school musical.

While it all felt strange, Miriam leaned back in her seat and smiled. Sixth grade would be so much better once she had a part in the musical. The first few weeks at a new school had been so hard only "knowing" Stephanie, who sat four rows behind her on the bus. She saw Stephanie in choir and at lunch, but there was no room at her table for Miriam at lunch. Miriam usually just sat at the table where everyone who sat there was sitting by themselves. She brought a book to read to make it look like that's what she wanted to do at lunch. Everyone had been friends since Kindergarten around here, and she was the new girl. She would finally be able to make some friends during rehearsals. Tryouts were in one week, and they would be getting the script and music for tryouts today in music. Her wish would make life so much better.

Miriam barely paid attention in any of her classes that day except for music. She kept wondering about the island and her grandmother's experience there. In music, she finally got to find out what musical they would be doing — A Grimm Experience. The show would go through several of the Grimm brothers' fairy tales, and each would have a song. Two main characters were in every scene and had a few solo parts — the narrators. They would represent the Grimm brothers and take the audience through the tales. That was the part Miriam wanted. She looked around the room to see if she could pick out who would be good as the other narrator, but she still didn't know anyone very well after being in school for less than two months. There wasn't much time to talk with anyone in classes, but now they would have to practice lines and parts. She and the other narrator would probably have to have separate practice times. Miriam knew this was how she would finally make friends. Mrs. Bell, the choir teacher, told them they would all sing the same song for tryouts, and then she would assign parts. Tryouts were during class all next week. Miriam carefully tucked the script and tryout song selection in her backpack when the bell rang. She would start practicing as soon as she got home.

Miriam tried not to think about the island or her grandmother on the bus ride home. Her grandmother wouldn't be home until dinnertime — she went to swimming classes at a local gym on Mondays, Wednesdays, and Fridays. On Tuesdays and Thursdays, she had her walking group at the mall. The weekend rotated between Master Gardeners, volunteering with the historical society, or the library's book club. She loved that her grandmother was active, but it was different than what she had been used to with her aunt and uncle — and even her parents. Her aunt or uncle were almost always home when she was home. If they needed a sitter, they took her to her grandmother's house. They told her they didn't want to leave her alone much until she was at least ten, but Miriam thought they just got into the habit of always being with her. Her grandmother thought a 11-year-old was old enough to be home alone.

"When I was that age, I was working after school at the library or my friends and I played outside after dinner until it was dark," Grandma told her aunt and uncle one day when they came to pick her up, and Grandma was just coming home from her swimming class. "Miriam is perfectly fine here by herself. There's a yard, TV, books, and a phone."

Miriam put her backpack down by the front door when she got home and took an apple from the refrigerator. She grabbed the sheet music for the musical from her backpack and took it to the piano in the formal dining room. Miriam didn't remember the last time anyone actually ate in there; holiday meals were usually held at her parents' or her aunt and uncle's house growing up. One end of the table had a sewing machine, and the other had some paperwork from the historical society that Grandma was organizing. Miriam had a section of the table that was hers to do homework and work on projects. At the far end of the room, across from the doorway to the kitchen, was an old, small piano. Several keys were chipped, but it was in tune. Grandma occasionally played when she was "in the mood," but Miriam hadn't touched it since she moved in. She had taken piano lessons for a year before her parents died, and her aunt and uncle had her keep taking them until they started getting ready to move. When they sold their keyboard, she was done with lessons. They said she could take them again when she moved in with her grandmother, but Miriam didn't really want to, so she didn't ask her about lessons. She knew enough to read the sheet music in front of her so she could practice the song. That was good enough for her. She ate the apple with her left hand and picked out the notes with her right hand. Once she had played it over a few times and the melody was stuck in her head, she threw the apple core in the trash and started singing the song.

Come along with us

to a world full of tales

the Grimm brothers wrote

to which your life will pale:

Red Riding Hood, the Billy Goats Gruff,

Rapunzel, Cinderella, Hansel and Gretel,

Rumpelstiltskin, Snow White,

Tom Thumb — so put on a kettle.

Enjoy the stories as they come alive

and take them to heart

for each one has a lesson.

Now the show must start!

It was an easy tune to pick up for Miriam. She would sing it over and over every day. She already felt confident she would be chosen for the part. She would work hard, but her wish had to come true, too, right? She was still singing the song at the piano when Grandma came home. She didn't hear the garage door, so Miriam was startled when she felt her grandmother's hand on her shoulder.

"That sounds lovely, Miriam," she said. "Oh, I didn't mean to startle you. Is that the song for the musical?"

"Yes! Do you like it? I'm going to practice it every day, so I can get one of the lead parts."

"It's fun and catchy. What is the musical going to be about? Did I hear Rapunzel in the song?"

"It's going to have Rapunzel in it, but it's going to be about several Grimm brothers' fairy tales. There are two narrators who get to talk and sing in about every scene. I want to be one!"

"That would be a fun part. When are the tryouts, and what do you have to do?"

"Next week during class. I have to sing this song and then say some of the lines from the show that the teacher will pick that day. I have the entire script, though."

"I'd like to see that — maybe after dinner? I'm making us tacos tonight, and I even found some avocados for guacamole. Want to help me?"

"Sure," Miriam said and followed her into the kitchen. She was humming the song as she walked.

"Wait! I almost forgot — you have to tell me about the island!" Miriam said as they sat down to eat dinner. She hit her forehead with her hand. She couldn't believe she went so long without asking her grandma about it. She had been so sidetracked with the new musical song.

Grandma smiled but took a bite of her taco before saying a word.

"I know all about Orphan Wish Island. When I was 12, I was living with my aunt and uncle. My father had died in the war when I was only four, and my mother had a heart attack at work when I was six. My aunt and uncle adopted me. I don't know if you remember your great-grandmother who lived in the nursing home when you were little, but that was actually my aunt."

"I didn't realize you lost your parents when you were little, too," Miriam said. She had only nibbled on one chip when her grandmother started her story.

"I was very little and don't really remember them much. My aunt and uncle were good about keeping photos, stories, and mementos for me, but they were also okay with me calling them mom and dad. My two older cousins started considering me more of a sibling as time went on, too.

"It was a few days after my 12th birthday when I saw the writing on my bedroom door," she put her hand in front of her face with a finger pointing out like she was tracing letters. "On a full moon, when the lights blink three, the door will connect to your family tree. Only orphans may enter and find what they seek. Open the door. Be brave, not meek."

"That's what it said on the attic door!" Miriam said. Grandma had closed her eyes as she said the poem.

"I still remember what my parents said that first night." Miriam waited for Grandma to tell her what they said, but she just stayed quiet for a few minutes. Miriam ate a few bites of her taco and waited on her grandma to open her eyes. Knowing how many times she had already replayed her parents' conversation in her head, she knew the memories of it were precious.

When Grandma opened her eyes, they were wet.

"Amazing how much you can miss people you barely even knew," she said in a quiet voice. She sighed and dipped a chip in the guacamole bowl.

"Did you make any wishes?" Miriam asked.

"Yes, but I only went back for two years. It's one of my few regrets in life. I wish I had gone back to hear my parents' final message. But I didn't think my wish was granted the second year, so I didn't go back.

"The first year, I wished to make the basketball team and be a point guard. I practiced every day and was voted the Most Valuable Player that year. I think the trophy is still in a box upstairs. The second year, I really wanted a puppy. I knew my aunt was allergic to dogs, but I just knew somehow it would work out. I saw a sign for free puppies one day at the grocery store and brought one home. My aunt tried for almost a week to live with the dog, but she was having trouble sleeping, and sneezing all the time. We had to take him to the pound. She said that if I wanted a dog so much, I should have asked, and they could have researched dogs that didn't shed. I'm guessing my parents wanted me to learn some responsibility that year, but all I could feel was devastation that I couldn't have the one thing that I wanted when I didn't even have my parents. I was mad for months and months. When the door glowed after my 14th birthday, I just rolled over and went to sleep. It never glowed again."

"Oh, Grandma, I'm so sorry."

"Well, that's my story, and you don't have to be sorry. I did learn a very valuable lesson and apologized to my aunt. Your story will be different, though. What did you wish for?"

"I wished to be the lead in the school musical," Miriam said. "I'm going to work hard and practice. I think I'll make more friends doing it, too."

"That's a good wish. That's like my basketball wish," Grandma smiled and reached over and patted Miriam's arm. "I'll have to get that trophy down to show you this week."

They finished up dinner without talking too much. Miriam did the dishes, and Grandma packed Miriam's lunch for the next day. They talked about their days and watched a cooking competition show before Miriam headed up to her room to finish her homework and get ready for bed. When Miriam went to say goodnight to her grandmother, she found her already asleep in the recliner. She then realized that Grandma had not asked her about what her parents had said to her.

"I made it! I made it!" Miriam shouted as soon as her grandma came home from her swimming class. Tryouts had gone well, and Mrs. Bell had posted the casting list after school today — one week after tryouts. To Miriam, the past two weeks had felt like they took forever to get through.

"Congratulations!" Grandma dropped her gym bag by the door and hugged Miriam tightly. "Did anyone else you know get good parts?"

"I don't really know many in the class yet, but the other narrator seems really nice — Sydney Harrington."

"That's good because you'll probably have to practice with her a lot."

"Stephanie next door is going to be Little Red Riding Hood," Miriam added.

"Oh, I didn't realize Stephanie was interested in the musical. That will be nice, too. I think we should go out and celebrate tonight. Want to pick the restaurant?"

"That would be fun, Grandma! Can we go to Garbo's? I feel like a big plate of spaghetti and meatballs with breadsticks. I was so nervous waiting for the results, I didn't eat much lunch today. Can I get cheesecake for dessert, too?"

"Sure. That sounds good. Let me take a quick shower and change and then we'll head out. Maybe you could send your aunt and uncle an email about the musical while you wait."

Miriam had told her aunt and uncle she would email them a few times a week when they left for Kenya. They wrote her a long email every weekend. She knew they would be excited about her getting the narrator's role, but every time she sat down to email them, she started missing them and then missing her parents even more. She had only written them once or twice a month since moving in with her grandma. She took her backpack up to her room and unpacked her homework for the night. She only had a few math problems and science and social studies worksheets.

She pulled out the musical script and decided to highlight her parts as Narrator 1. She could email her aunt and uncle later.

During music class the next day, Mrs. Bell broke them into small groups to practice scenes so they could work on their lines. They would alternate days when they would work on lines and work on the music. The entire class would sing all the songs, but certain characters had solo or duet parts. Mrs. Bell said she would work on those in a few weeks. They had four months until their performance in mid-February, right before spring break. Mrs. Bell said she liked to start practicing early because they would lose practice time with Thanksgiving and winter breaks.

Miriam and Sydney moved to a corner of the room to start working on their lines.

"So, you're pretty new here, right?" Sydney asked Miriam as they sat on the floor with their scripts in their laps.

"I was at a school over on the Kansas side for the last few years when I lived with my aunt and uncle," Miriam replied. "They went to be missionaries in Kenya, so I now live with my grandma."

"You don't live with your parents?"

Miriam took a deep breath. She hated it when people asked about her parents. Once they knew her parents were dead, people often acted weird around her or seemed to pity her. She thought she'd give Sydney a chance, though. She was really hoping they would be good friends.

"My parents both died in a car accident when I was almost eight years old," Miriam said quietly. She didn't want anyone else in the room to hear, although she was sure Mrs. Bell knew.

"Oh, no!" Sydney said. She reached over and put her hand on Miriam's arm. "That has to be so hard. It's not the same, but my baby brother died a few years ago just a few days after he was born. I still get sad sometimes."

"I do, too," Miriam said. "I'm sorry about your brother. This will sound strange, but I'm glad you understand."

"I'm glad to find someone who understands, too," Sydney replied. "My friends were very supportive when it happened, but they don't like me to talk about it anymore, and they don't want to go to the cemetery with me anymore. I like to go once a month and tell him what's going on. I don't have any other brothers or sisters. I really wanted one, but my parents don't want to try again."

"I'd go with you if you want," Miriam said. Just then, Mrs. Bell stopped by them.

"Are you girls working on your lines? You seem to be talking quite a bit."

"We were just getting to know each other better first," Sydney spoke up. "We'll get started now."

They worked on their lines for the rest of the class. They worked very well together and swapped phone numbers and addresses. They lived only four blocks from each other, so they could walk or bike to each other's houses.

Miriam was telling her grandmother all about her conversation with Sydney while they ate dinner, when the phone rang. Grandma wouldn't answer the phone during dinner but checked the voicemail as Miriam cleared the dishes.

"It's for you," Grandma said. "Sydney wants you to spend the night in two weeks."

"Can I? She lives just four blocks away."

"What did you say her last name was?"

"Harrington."

"I think I might know her dad from the historical society. I think that should be fine, but let me talk to her mom or dad before you hang up."

"Okay, Grandma. Thank you!"

Miriam called Sydney back, and she picked up just after two rings.

"Harrington's. Sydney here."

"Sydney, it's Miriam. I got your message."

"Can you spend the night next Friday? I told my parents we could practice our lines. I would ask you for this Friday, but we have a family birthday dinner for my grandma in the city."

"I can, but my grandma wants to talk to one of your parents before she gives the final yes. She thinks she may know your dad from the historical society."

"Yep, that's my dad. He's a World War I history buff. I'll get him."

Miriam handed the phone to her grandmother and listened as they talked about the historical society chili cook-off coming up next month. When she finally got the phone back, Grandma told her the sleepover was okay with her.

"Sydney?"

"I'm here. Guess we know not to get them started on history stuff again. Not my favorite topic."

"Not mine either. The sleepover is a go, though!"

"Great! See you in class tomorrow."

"Bye."

Miriam smiled as she hung up the phone. All her wishes were coming true. Could this really be all her parents and the Volturians doing, or would these things have happened anyway?

Chapter 4

The next day, Sydney waved Miriam over to her table at lunch, and she was introduced to Sydney's friends — Anna, Michelle, Karen, and Grace. They all lived on the same block and had been friends since preschool. Anna was in music with them, and her long hair was probably what won her the role of Rapunzel. She had math and science with Michelle and Grace, and English with Karen. Michelle wore Disney clothes every day and had a Minnie Mouse backpack. Miriam learned that Grace was very smart, and she wore turquoise glasses. Karen had already been caught twice this year reading a book during English class when the teacher was talking to them about grammar. They asked her a ton of questions about her aunt and uncle and what they did in Kenya, but none of them asked about her parents. Sydney must have already told them about it. At least they would understand somewhat, having been friends with Sydney when her brother died.

"What house do you live in?" Karen asked. "I know a couple people who live on Monroe Street."

"It's the white house with a swing on the front porch and a balcony off the second story in front. There are a lot of trees blocking the front of the house, but you can see the porch. It's right across from the cemetery," Miriam said.

"Wait," Grace said. "That's right next door to Stephanie Risner, isn't it?"

"Yes, she lives next door," Miriam replied.

They all looked at each other, and Miriam wondered if the news about Stephanie living next door to her was good or bad.

"What?" Miriam asked.

"Stephanie used to be friends with us," Michelle said. "Then, she became a peewee cheerleader in fourth grade and stopped talking to us. She thinks she's with the 'cool' kids, but they're all just cheerleaders together, and that's all they do."

"I've only talked to her a few times, but she's never been friendly or nice."

"That sounds like her," Sydney said. "Good thing you are starting to hang out with us instead, although if you're not into cheerleading, I doubt she would have hung out with you."

"Cheerleading is not my thing at all. I like soccer, singing, acting, and reading," Miriam said.

"You'll fit in with us just fine," Karen said and threw her arm around Miriam's shoulder.

Anna joined Miriam for the sleepover at Sydney's house. They made their own pizzas, baked chocolate chip cookies, watched a movie, and then read through the musical together. They took turns saying the roles that weren't theirs. Miriam and Sydney talked at the beginning and end of every scene and sometimes added a funny line here and there in the middle of the scenes. In Anna's scene as Rapunzel, Sydney came to the middle of the stage and said, "Now, this story would have been completely different had scissors been around in their kingdom in those days."

As Miriam finally laid down in her sleeping bag that night in Sydney's room, she could almost feel her parents smiling down at her from wherever they were. Did they wish she would make friends? Did they know she would end up living with her grandma and not with her aunt and uncle by the time she got to visit Orphan Wish Island? Miriam promised herself that night that she would go to the island every year. She had to know at the end what their wishes were for her and how they had come true — if they did. She wondered if she could ever tell her friends about the island. She'd have to ask Grandma about that. Or wait to see what the Volturians said about it next year. It felt like it would be a hard secret to keep, but then again, she wouldn't want her friends thinking she got things like the lead in the musical by wishing instead of by hard work.

"Did you know you talk in your sleep, Miriam?" Anna said the next morning as they were eating the pancakes Sydney's mom had made for them.

"No way," Miriam said.

"Oh, definitely," Sydney said. "Both Anna and I heard you talking about wishes. You woke us both up. You were talking about Starfruit, fairies, and wishes. It was just for a minute or two, then you went back to sleep."

"That's weird," Miriam said. She knew she couldn't give anything away to make the island sound real. "I think I dreamed about that stuff, but I can't believe I said stuff out loud. Sorry for waking you guys up."

"I'm fine with it," Anna said. "About once a month, one of my little brothers sleepwalks into my room. I just lead him back to bed and then go back to bed myself. I fell right back asleep when you were done talking."

"It took me a while to fall back asleep," Sydney said. "I was fascinated, though. That was the first time I've heard someone talk in their sleep."

"You'll have to record me next time," Miriam said, laughing. "I've never heard anyone talk in their sleep either — and I'd love to know what I said."

"We just might do that," Sydney said. She and Anna joined in the laughter.

The next few months went by quickly with extra musical practices twice a week after school for her and Sydney. One was to review lines, and the other was to work on their duets. Sydney sang the soprano part, and Miriam sang alto. The songs were pretty basic, so they got them down rather quickly. Sydney and her friends all had rather large family gatherings to attend at both Thanksgiving and Christmas. Miriam and her grandma spent both with friends of Grandma's who had no other family nearby. Miriam enjoyed helping Grandma host both dinners at the house. Her aunt and uncle called both days, and at Thanksgiving, she told them about the musical. She hadn't emailed them. She blamed being so busy with the musical, but she wanted to adjust to life with her grandma and not think about how much she missed living with her aunt and uncle and her old friends from her old school.

Her friends had all said they would call and hang out when she said goodbye to them last summer, but so far, only Olivia had emailed her once to say hi right before school started. Miriam had emailed back, but Olivia never responded. Miriam knew she could call them, too, but she had hoped they would miss her as much as she missed them. She decided to send a mass email to all her old friends over Christmas break and ask them to come to her musical. Maybe, just maybe, at least one of them would come and see her.

They would perform the musical four times — once during school on Friday for an assembly, once Friday night, and then Saturday afternoon and evening. There was a cast party Sunday afternoon at Sydney's house, which had a big basement with a large television, pool table, darts, ping-pong, and a small kitchen. Most of the sleepovers with her friends were held at her house because since she didn't have any siblings, and they always had the basement to themselves.

The Thursday before the first performance, they had a final dress rehearsal after school. Anna's mom was there with her sewing kit and sewing machine in case any of the costumes needed to be fixed. Miriam and Sydney both wore top hats, black pants and vests, a white button-up shirt, and held notebooks with quill pens. They had been allowed to wear any color of shoes, so they had gone shopping a few weeks ago and bought sparkly tennis shoes. Miriam chose emerald green, and Sydney chose dark purple. They knew the spotlight would make them stand out. Mrs. Bell complimented their choice when she saw them that night.

"Ask Anna's mom if she could add some sequins of the same color to your hats," she told them.

"Okay," Sydney replied. They asked Mrs. Garrison. She said she actually had some sequins in those colors left over from a peacock Halloween costume she had made Anna three years ago. They gave her their hats and headed back to the stage to get ready for the rehearsal.

"Are you excited or nervous?" Sydney asked her as they walked behind the maroon curtain.

"Both," Miriam said.

"Me, too, but it should be fun, right?" Sydney said.

"It should. Well, break a leg!" Miriam said.

"You, too. Break a leg," Sydney said, and they headed to opposite sides of the stage.

"Okay, everyone, we're going to take it from the top," Mrs. Bell said. "I'll do a quick announcement, then you know the cue to start when the song comes on."

The dress rehearsal and all four performances went great. They got a standing ovation at each performance, even though almost everyone messed up a line or a note at some point over the weekend. Miriam realized on Saturday night that she loved being on the stage. Even when she messed up and called Little Red Riding Hood Rapunzel on Friday night, she ad-libbed and said, "Oh, wait, that's your cousin, not you," when she realized her mistake. The crowd laughed, and she was glad she hadn't gotten flustered. Her grandma sat in the front row for each performance and recorded the Saturday night one. She posted it on a web site on Sunday so Miriam's aunt and uncle could watch it while Miriam was at the cast party. Everyone at the party congratulated her on the ad-lib and her overall performance. She stuck with Anna and Sydney for most of the party but tried to talk to a few other kids there. *I might be doing several shows over the years with these kids*, she thought. After trying some sports and piano lessons, she had finally found an activity she really enjoyed. She knew that when she went to junior high next year, there was a drama club that put on musicals and plays. She would join that and sign up for choir. Despite moving to a new school, Miriam felt like sixth grade was going to end up being quite a successful year.

Miriam spent most of the summer pondering what she should wish for when she visited the island in October. Her friends were only in town a week or two here or there, going on vacations to Florida, California, and Canada. She got to go to Lincoln and Omaha for a family reunion, but she mostly helped her grandma with the garden and projects around the house. And, she decided to give Stephanie another chance.

Stephanie went outside almost every day around 2 p.m. to get the mail. Miriam could see her from her window seat in her room. She knew Stephanie couldn't see her because she had looked up to her room from the sidewalk and the tree branches blocked most of the view. Miriam knew the exact spot to look to see the street. Miriam hadn't seen any of Stephanie's friends come by at all since school let out. She asked Grandma one night if the Risners went on vacation. Grandma said she doubted it. Mr. Risner was a doctor who delivered babies, and women paid a premium to have him as their doctor because he was always on call for them. His wife was a realtor who worked nights and weekends a lot. Her grandma said Stephanie had a live-in nanny until she was about 10 and her parents thought she could handle being on her own. The day after she learned that information about Stephanie, she decided to go over and say hi. There was a new movie on television that night, and Grandma said she could invite people over to watch it if she wanted. All of her friends were out of town, so Stephanie was the last option.

She walked up the front yard sidewalk and noticed the lawn had diagonal marks. A lawn company came by Stephanie's house about twice a week, while Miriam and her grandma took turns mowing their lawn. There were three concrete stairs leading up to the dark green front door, which stood out against the light brown siding that was supposed to look like wood. Miriam rang the doorbell and waited. She rang it a second time and was about to leave when the door finally opened. Even though it was after noon, Stephanie looked like she had just woken up. She was dressed in the school's cheer sweatpants and a T-shirt from a cheer camp with her blonde hair pulled back in a messy ponytail.

"Oh, hi," Stephanie said. "Whatever you're selling, my parents probably already bought it from someone at work."

"Actually, Stephanie," Miriam said as Stephanie started to close the door. "I'm not here to sell anything. I was wondering if you'd like to come over later today and watch a movie with me. It's the new one with Tom Smithe."

"Um, what?" Stephanie said, putting her hands on her hips. "Don't you have one of the nerdy girls to hang out with?"

"I don't know what you mean by nerdy, but if you're talking about my friends, they're all on vacation right now. I thought maybe we could hang out sometimes since you live next door, and we have the next six years of junior/senior high together."

"I'm sorry you need more friends, Miri, but I have enough. Plus, I've already seen that movie in the theater three times."

"A simple no would have been fine, Steph. I don't need more friends — I have plenty. But I noticed none of yours have stopped by yet this summer."

"Well, that's only because I'm not supposed to have people over when my parents aren't home, which they hardly ever are."

"Well, okay then. If you change your mind, I'm right next door."

"I won't." Stephanie shut the door, and Miriam started walking back to her house. She'd never had anyone talk to her like that before. She remembered something her aunt used to say when they saw bullies or mean people in TV shows or movies. "I usually feel bad for people who are that mean — it means they're really unhappy with their life."

As Miriam went upstairs to get her book so she could read in the hammock in the backyard, she thought about how it couldn't be fun for Stephanie to never spend time with her parents. Miriam had a good reason for her parents to not be around. Stephanie did not. While life was hard with her parents gone, Miriam realized she never felt unloved. Her aunt, uncle, and grandma had taken good care of her and let her grieve and reminisce and keep her parents as part of her life. If she never saw them because they were working ...

Splash! Miriam was suddenly covered in water, and her book was soaked. She quickly got out of the hammock and saw the blue remains of a water balloon. She heard a door close at Stephanie's house behind the fence. Miriam didn't care that her clothes or hair were all wet, but the book she was holding was a library book, and she'd have to pay for the damage.

"I'll get you back for this, Steph," Miriam said under her breath, all sympathy for Stephanie gone.

Chapter 5

Seventh-grade orientation was held a week before school started. Miriam and her grandma arrived at the junior high gym just a few minutes before it started. The bleacher seats were almost full, and they had to sit near the front in the middle. Before she sat down, she waved to Anna, Michelle, and Grace, who were sitting at the top. She noticed that Stephanie was seated just a few rows behind them with her mother. Her mother had long, straight blond hair, and that was about all Miriam could see of her since she was looking down at her phone and typing away. Stephanie was chatting with three other cheerleaders who were sitting beside her. Miriam knew from Anna, who had a brother going into 11th grade, that there would be a welcome speech in the gymnasium, and then students would get their schedules and locker assignments and could go find out where they were. They would also be able to see all the after-school clubs they could join. Parents and guardians would stay and chat in the gymnasium and find their kids when they were ready to leave.

A woman wearing black pants and a red dress shirt with a limp bow at the top walked up to the podium in the middle of the gym floor. The podium had the school's mascot on the front — a Bearcat. Bristolway Bearcats was written in a circle around the bearcat in the school colors, dark orange and dark brown.

"Good evening, Bearcats," she said in a commanding voice. "My name is Vanessa Traine, and I am the Principal of Bristolway Junior High School. Over there are our Vice Principal, Tom Ratcliff and our counselor, Everly Ozuma."

The Vice Principal and counselor were sitting off to the side of the gym and waved when they were introduced.

"School starts one week from today, and the teachers and staff are looking forward to having a great year with you! Tonight, you will get your schedules and locker assignments over to my left. There are several lines based on the first letter of your last name. Over to my right, there will be tables for all of our after-school clubs and sports. Please take the time to see all that is offered to you at Bristolway Junior High. The school is open for you to walk around and find your classrooms and lockers. Some teachers are in their rooms, so you and your parents can talk with them. All of our teachers' and staff's contact information can be found on our website in case you have questions or concerns. Mr. Ratcliff, Ms. Ozuma, and I will be available to answer any of your questions tonight, too.

"Before I let you go, I want to tell you about one exciting change at the school this year. We will be having a STEAM fair the week before spring break for the first time. It will be very similar to a science fair, but STEAM stands for Science, Technology, Engineering, Art and Mathematics. The students will be able to incorporate what they learn in all their classes into their projects. We will ask members of the community to come and be judges, and we will award prizes thanks to our PTO. They have a table by the front door with information on how parents can get involved.

"So, let's do a Bearcat cheer, then you can get ready to be Bristolway's newest seventh graders.

"Bristolway Bearcats — we are No. 1! Bristolway Bearcats — you can't stop the fun!"

The gym got very loud as the people in the bleachers shouted the cheer.

"Do you mind if I go talk to Mrs. Smith while you get your schedule, Miri?" Grandma turned and asked her.

"Not at all," she responded. "I'll go find Sydney and the others. How about I meet you back here in an hour?"

"Sounds good. Oh, I see Mrs. Thompson here, too." Grandma waved to someone and walked off. Miriam was glad her grandma was so active and could be more like a parent to her. She couldn't imagine if she had to live with someone who acted like a really old lady.

Miriam started scanning the crowd for Sydney when she heard Stephanie talking really loudly as she walked down the bleacher stairs with her friends.

"My uncle works for NASA down in Houston," she said. "That STEAM project is going to be a guaranteed blue ribbon for me. Maybe if you're really nice to me this year, I can ask him to help you guys out some, too."

"Oh, Steph, you'll for sure win if he helps you," a girl with red, curly hair said. Miriam didn't know her name. "I've never been good at science and math. I'll need your help for sure."

Miriam spotted Sydney and Anna and started walking toward them. She couldn't hear Stephanie and her friends anymore. As she walked, she decided she knew exactly what to wish for this fall. She smiled as she thought it over — her real wish would be to beat Stephanie, but would just say she wanted to win the STEAM fair. It would be great to see Stephanie's face when even her NASA uncle's help couldn't get her what she wanted.

After they all got their schedules, Miriam and her friends compared them and their locker assignments. Their lockers were all in Hallway F except for Michelle and Sydney, but theirs were just around the corner in Hallway E. Miriam and Anna had music together again. Michelle was in her homeroom and math class. Karen was in reading and social studies with her. Grace was in her science class. No one was in her special rotation class with her (art, gym, life skills, and library), and Sydney wasn't in any of her classes. They all had a friend with them for all but one or two classes.

"We'll have to all join one after-school club together," Michelle said. She was wearing a headband that had small mouse ears on it. "Let's go and see what they offer."

There was art club, newspaper club, book club, chess club, math club, library club, kindness club, writing club, and craft club. Karen was going to try out for volleyball, Michelle wanted to play basketball, and Sydney was going to try out for soccer, but none of those were fall sports.

"Let's go check out Kindness Club," Karen said. "That sounds like it could be fun."

The Kindness Club representative was a boy with wavy brown hair that went down past his ears.

"Are you girls interested in Kindness Club?" he asked.

"Can you tell us what you do in Kindness Club?" Karen asked in return.

"Kindness Club is a group of kids that like to find ways to do random acts of kindness. We have a suggestion box where people can leave us a note to let us know if they or someone else is having a hard time, and we try to find some way to cheer them up. For example, when Lucas broke his leg last year and had to get around for a few weeks in a wheelchair, students in the Kindness Club helped him get from class to class and carry his things. We also found ways to help him decorate his wheelchair and made a ramp to the football bleachers so he could sit with his friends at the games."

"That sounds great!" Anna said. She turned to the group. "Should we sign up?"

"Yes!" they all said in unison.

"We meet on Mondays after school and Fridays during lunch. You only have to come to two meetings a month to be part of the club and do one random act of kindness a week," the boy said. "Our first meeting is next Friday in Mrs. Grayson's room — she's the art teacher." He handed each of them a flyer with all the same information he had told them.

"See you Friday," he said as they walked away. Miriam looked at the clock on the gym wall and saw it was about time for her to meet up with Grandma. She said goodbye to her friends and went off to find her. She was looking forward to this year.

Grandma agreed that she could invite all five girls over for a sleepover for her birthday. Even though her birthday was on a Saturday, she had the sleepover on Friday, wanting to make sure she was available all day Sunday in case the door opened to the island. They were going to have a spa night and watch *Star Wars* movies. They were taking a popcorn-making break when the doorbell rang. Grandma had already gone to bed, so Miriam answered the door. She peeked through the peephole and saw it was Stephanie. She was crying and holding something in her hands.

"Please help me," Stephanie said as soon as Miriam opened the door. "I found it this afternoon and tried to feed it, but it's not moving anymore. My parents won't answer their phones."

Miriam stepped out onto the front patio to look at what Stephanie was holding. Her friends started to come to the door behind her. It was a tiny squirrel, and it wasn't moving much at all.

"What does she want, Miriam?" Anna said behind her. Stephanie looked up and seemed very surprised to see the girls standing behind Miriam.

"It's okay, Steph," Miriam said. "We'll help you. Girls, she has a baby squirrel that isn't doing well. It's hardly moving. Anyone know of a place that helps squirrels that's open at 10 p.m.?"

"Actually, I do," Karen said. "My mom volunteers at the Hopewell Animal Haven over in Kansas a few times a month. They take any animal native to our area, and they have an emergency number."

"Stephanie, come on in," Miriam said as she led Stephanie into the house and into the kitchen. "Karen, can you find that number? My laptop is on top of the piano."

"What's all this racket?" Miriam's grandma said as she came out of the hallway in her faded green bathrobe, still squinting her eyes.

"Sorry, Grandma," Miriam said. "Stephanie found a baby squirrel that's not doing well. We're finding the number to the Hopewell Animal Haven to come help it."

"Are your parents home, Stephanie?"

"No, they're at some hospital awards banquet and not answering their phones," she said. She was still cuddling the squirrel in a light blue hand towel.

"Let me see it," Grandma said. She gently took the squirrel from Stephanie and lightly ran her finger from its head to its tail down its back. Then she gently put her finger on its chest. "It's still breathing. It may just be sleeping, but it's too small for you to care for on your own. We should call Hopewell. I remember reading about them taking in a baby squirrel last year. It now spends most of the day on one of the worker's shoulders as she goes about her work there. Very cute."

Grandma put her arm on Stephanie's shoulder, and Stephanie seemed to relax some. Miriam realized Stephanie had been really worried about the little animal.

Karen called Hopewell, and they told her there was a volunteer who lived only 10 minutes away who could come pick up the squirrel. They said to give him up to an hour before calling back to check. It was only 20 minutes later that a tall, lanky man in workout clothes showed up to get the squirrel.

"Thanks, ladies, for watching out for this little guy. Who found him?"

"I did," Stephanie said. She stepped forward. "Can I say goodbye?"

"Sure," he said. "How exactly did you find him?"

"I was walking around the backyard and heard something in the leaves around one of our trees. When I looked closer, there it was, just lying on the ground. I looked around for a nest or other squirrels for almost an hour before I picked it up. I tried to give it a little milk like I saw on the Internet, but he didn't like it. He hasn't moved much since I picked him up around 4 p.m., but then around 9 p.m., it seemed like he wasn't even breathing."

"Sounds like he fell out of a nest, but it's strange for a momma squirrel to not check on her babies for an hour. Can I come back tomorrow to see if there are any more babies around?"

"Sure, I live next door," she said and pointed to her house.

"Well, here's my card. Have your parents give me a call in the morning and I'll come over," he said. "Thanks again. Oh, did you name the little guy?"

"Flufftail," Stephanie said quietly.

"Good name," he said and then left.

After he had gone, Grandma took Stephanie outside and watched her walk home safely.

"What a night!" she said when she came back in. She was smiling. "I'm going to bed now — again. Try to keep the excitement down a little bit."

"We will," Miriam said. "Goodnight, Grandma."

They all stayed pretty quiet until they heard Grandma's door close.

"Wow," Sydney said. "That's the most I've talked to Stephanie in three years. She did always love animals."

"I wonder if she'll let us talk to her on Monday," Anna said. "It would be nice to hang out with her again."

"We'll just have to see," Karen said. "Ready to watch more of the movie? I still can't believe Michelle hasn't seen this one all the way through."

"I know every Disney movie by heart, though," Michelle said.

At breakfast Sunday morning, Miriam told Grandma that she hoped the door would open tonight to the island.

"It's very exciting," Grandma said. "I hope you've thought of a good wish."

"I have," Miriam said. "I want to ..."

"No! Don't tell me," she interrupted. "I don't want to have any influence on trying to make the wish come true. Tell me when you go back the next year and how it comes true. If it's something that will help you and that your parents want to happen, it will come true. I know you told me about your wish to have a lead in the musical, but there wasn't much I could do to influence that one. I would hate to accidentally do something that makes your wish not come true."

"Oh, good thought," Miriam replied. "I'm glad I can talk to you about the island, though."

"I am, too," Grandma said. "I think that may be part of why I didn't go back after two years. Without being able to talk about it, it didn't seem real."

"You're sure you don't want me to tell you what I plan to wish for?" Miriam asked.

"I'm sure. Now eat your birthday pancakes so we can get to church."

Miriam had spent most of the day in her room, just in case the writing on the door showed up early. She hurried back up to her room right after dinner that night. She sat in the window seat like she did the previous year and opened her book to her place. She looked closely at the bookmark from her parents and noticed that behind the kittens playing with string were stars and palm trees. She didn't remember looking that hard at the bookmark before, but they seemed new. Miriam started reading where she left off but had trouble concentrating. She tried to remember times with her parents. She closed her book and stared out the window as she thought about the time they went to Denver and spent a whole day in the Museum of Natural History. She remembered they went somewhere for dinner afterward, and she had spaghetti and then fell asleep at the table. It was the summer before she turned seven. She remembered that when she entered the room with the Tyrannosaurus Rex skeleton, she stopped and stared. She was a little scared but didn't want to show it. She felt her dad grab her hand and lean down to whisper something to her. "Itty bitty arms," he said, and they both laughed. She loved looking at the dinosaurs after that. Her mom loved looking at the Egyptian history exhibit.

Miriam was thinking about the sarcophaguses when she saw the street lamps blink across the street. They blinked three times in quick succession and then did it again about a minute later. Then, the power went out, and Miriam saw the writing appear on the attic door. She stood up and put the book down on the window seat. She paused a second as she put her hand on the doorknob. "It's not just a dream," she said as she closed her eyes and opened the door. When the door was wide open, she opened her eyes. It was there! Orphan Wish Island was there! She stepped onto the island and shut the door.

She took her time walking toward the group of other teens in the middle of the island. There were only four others there this time. There was a gentle breeze that blew her hair across her face. She moved it and looked up at the sky — not a cloud in sight. It was the perfect temperature on the island. She wished she could spend a week there and just enjoy a break. There was so much more homework in seventh grade. It felt like she rarely had any downtime with school, drama club, and Kindness Club.

"Hi, everyone," Miriam said. "Any fairies yet?"

"We're not fairies!" a voice said behind her. Miriam looked over her shoulder to see the yellow fairy. She remembered her name was Stella.

"You're right," Miriam said. "You do look like them, though."

Stella laughed, then counted them out. "One, two, three, four... there's supposed to be five. Have any of you seen Elaine yet?"

"I was here first, and there's only been us four show up," the boy said. His hair was dyed blue at the tips this year.

"Thank you, Aaron," Stella said. "Well, we'll just get started, and I'll wait a little bit to see if she shows up. The door will only be open until midnight where she lives. Did everyone enjoy their wishes this year?"

"It was a really great year," the girl with red hair said. "I know exactly what to wish for this year."

"Same for me," Miriam said.

"Okay, then — don't let me get in your way," Stella said. "Feel free to grab the Starfruit with your name on it from the tree you planted and make your wish. It works the same as last year. You can hear the same message from your parents if you want. Also, don't forget to bury your fruit under your tree after you take a bite and make your wish."

The red-headed girl beat Miriam to the tree, but she was close behind. Miriam saw that Aaron was talking to Stella, and he looked like he was arguing with her. She looked back at the fruit in her hand with her name on it and walked a few feet away from everyone, sat down, and closed her eyes before taking a bite. She wanted to hear her parents' voices again.

"We are so glad you decided to come to this island," her mother said. "We know it can't be easy without us there to help you grow up, but we made wishes that we hope will help you as you become an adult."

"We can't tell you what we wished for until you turn 18. They're all good, though!" her dad said. "We hope you make good wishes, too."

"We can't be there to see you. We had to make these wishes before heading on to Heaven. This is a recorded message."

"But," her dad continued, "they said if you make your wish each year, we can meet you when you come back at 18. I can't wait to see what a beautiful young lady you turn into!"

"We love you more than the world! Be good and be kind," her mom said.

"And be smart, Miribug," her dad said. "Bye."

A few tears rolled down Miriam's cheeks. It felt like they were right there with her, but she knew when she opened her eyes, they wouldn't be there. She took a deep breath and made her wish.

"I wish to win the STEAM fair this year," she whispered with her eyes still closed. She replayed the message from her parents one more time before opening her eyes and standing up. All the others were already burying their fruit, so Miriam walked over and joined them.

"I hope it works this time," she heard Aaron mumble. He stood up and started walking away before Miriam could ask him what he meant. Could his wish have not come true? They had to come true, didn't they? Unless he wished for something that they weren't supposed to wish for...

"Everything okay?" Stella said as she hovered a few feet above the ground by Miriam.

"I think so. Did Aaron's wish not come true?"

"It did, but not in the way he pictured in his head. Remember, your parents made wishes for you, too, so the two wishes have to blend together."

"Oh, well, I hope he's happier about what happens this next year. Where are the other two fai... Volturians?"

"They're busy today at other islands. There are many Orphan Wish Islands for different countries and years. We usually only have more than one of us when it's the welcoming year."

Miriam scanned the horizon for other islands but could only see the ocean.

"Oh, you can't see the other islands. You can only see yours. Ready to go home?"

"I guess so. I could spend a week here — it's so perfect. But life awaits."

"Very true. I hope to see you next year. Tell Peggy I said hi and that her parents wished for peace for her heart."

Stella quickly flew over to the only other girl left — the one with long, blond hair. Miriam started walking to her door and wondered what her grandma would think about the message from Stella. She turned back and took one more look over the island before stepping back into her bedroom. What a wonderful place to exist!

She entered her room and closed the door to the attic. She quickly opened it again, hoping she could still get to the island, but all she saw was darkness and boxes. She closed the door again and went to go tell her grandma the message from Stella, but she was fast asleep in her room, snoring. *I can tell her tomorrow*, Miriam thought. Miriam got ready for bed and started to lie down. Then, she had an idea. She opened the dresser draw with her socks in and found a picture frame tucked under all the socks. It was a picture of Miriam's parents taken the night they died. Her mom was wearing a dark blue sparkly dress and pearls, and her dad was wearing a suit with a blue and yellow-checkered tie. They were smiling, and her mom was leaning into her dad's shoulder. Some relative had printed it out, framed it, and had given it to her for the first Christmas without them. She had kept it on her desk for a few weeks but had put it away because it had made her miss them terribly every time she saw it. Now that she could hear their voices, she wanted to be able to see their faces. She put the photo on her nightstand and got into bed.

"Goodnight, Mom. Goodnight, Dad. Thank you for the wishes."

Then she turned off her lamp and went to sleep.

That night, she dreamed; a vivid dream of brilliant colors, fish, and plants. The sun shone through it all, and the whole scene shimmered brightly, like the Starfruit tree in the sun. Miriam woke up and remembered the dream and knew right away what her project would be for the STEAM fair. She looked at the picture of her parents in the faint light of dawn and went back to sleep.

When Miriam's alarm went off, she quickly bounded down the stairs to tell her grandma the message from the island. She usually got dressed and ready before she went downstairs for breakfast, but she was excited to see how her grandma would react.

"Good morning," Grandma said. "You're down early."

"I have something to tell you! I went to the island last night! I made my wish, but before I left, Stella said to tell you hi and that your parents wished for peace for your heart."

Grandma stopped buttering the toast she had in her hand and turned her back to Miriam. Miriam walked over to her and put her hand on her arm.

"I always wondered ...," Grandma whispered. She looked at Miriam, and there were tears in her eyes. "Thank you."

She went back to buttering the toast. Miriam could sense her grandma needed some time by herself.

"I'll go finish getting ready and then come down and eat."

Grandma was quiet at breakfast but had a smile on her face when Miriam came back down. Miriam stayed quiet but gave her a big hug before she left for school.

Chapter 6

Halloween was on a Saturday that year, and while Miriam and her friends still wanted to dress up, they all felt too old to go trick-or-treating. Sydney talked her parents into hosting a party, and afterward, Anna, Michelle, Karen, Grace, and Miriam would stay the night. Sydney handed out small flyer invitations to other seventh graders at lunch a few days before. The very next day, another flyer started circulating inviting people to a party at Stephanie's house.

Sydney slammed down the orange flyer from Stephanie as she sat down at the lunch table.

"Can you believe this?" Sydney said. "And, after all we did to help her little squirrel!"

"Do you want to cancel yours?" Anna said.

"No way! I'm sure hers is going to have more people because she'll tell them her parents won't be there," Sydney replied.

"Wait," Miriam said. "I have an idea. We can have my grandma watch the party and call the cops if she notices anything crazy going on."

"Oh, that's a great idea," Michelle agreed.

"Or we could just call for her," Grace said. "But we have to make sure Steph doesn't call the cops on us."

"That doesn't matter — my parents will be at my house, and it'll just be a fun party," Sydney replied.

"I really think the best bet is to have my grandma complain. She's been worried about Steph after the squirrel incident and keeps an eye on the house when she's home," Miriam said.

"We'll go with that. Thanks, Miriam. Now, let's figure out what games we want to have at the party. My mom is buying a bunch of food today and even getting a cake that has all the characters we're dressing up as — Minnie, Belle, Hermione, Supergirl, a cat, and a rock star," Sydney told them.

"Cool!" Karen said. "Do you have plans for Twister?"

About 20 other seventh graders came to Sydney's party. Just as the last few were getting picked up after the four-hour get-together, Miriam heard police sirens heading past the house. She quickly found Sydney in the kitchen.

"Did you hear the sirens? I bet Grandma called the cops right before heading to bed. She can't stay up much past 10 any night," Miriam said.

"Yep, I bet she did. Our party was great, and hers is ending right now."

Sydney walked Miriam home the next morning after the other girls left. As they rounded the corner to Miriam's street, they noticed right away all the trash strewn across Steph's yard — and Steph was out in the yard picking it all up.

"Wasn't our party so much fun?" Sydney said loudly as they walked by Steph. Miriam knew right away what Sydney was doing.

"It was great — we may have to make that a new tradition," Miriam said just as loudly.

Sydney said bye to Miriam at her door, handing Miriam her purple sleeping bag, then started walking back home. Miriam watched her until she rounded the corner, just to make sure Steph didn't do or say anything mean. Steph just stared at her the whole time.

"Grandma, I'm home," Miriam called out as she walked into the house. Her grandma was reading the newspaper in her recliner and got up to help Miriam put her sleeping bag and overnight bag in her room. As they walked up the stairs, Grandma yawned.

"Tired?" Miriam asked.

"Yes, there was a party next door, and I had to call the police. I went over once to ask Steph to turn the music down and noticed a few open alcohol containers. She said her parents were home, but I know they were out at a fundraiser for the hospital last night. I tried calling her parents, but they didn't answer the phone. Luckily, the police came fairly quickly, and then I got some sleep."

"Yikes! I'm glad I went to Sydney's party," Miriam said. "It was just plain good fun."

"Me, too. I need to go get ready for a Master Gardener's meeting. Do you have anything you need to do today?"

"I have some homework, and I need to read more of *The City of Ember* since the book report is due in two weeks, and I want to practice piano. Probably take a nap, too. I'll be fine at home."

"Okay. I'll let you know before I head out, though."

Miriam collapsed on her bed when her Grandma left the room and smiled a huge smile. Their plan had worked. Steph's party had been ruined, and theirs had been great. *It's going to feel even better when I beat her at the STEAM fair*, Miriam thought.

A few days later at lunch, Karen sat down last at their table and told them she had some very interesting news to share.

"So, my mom came home last night and asked me if I saw Stephanie Risner much at school. I told her, 'Not really,' and then asked her why. She said that Stephanie was now volunteering at the Hopewell Animal Haven. Stephanie's mom is making her do community service as punishment for throwing the party. She has to volunteer 300 hours because there was thousands of dollars of damage to some furniture and carpet during the party!" Karen said.

"Yikes! That's a lot of damage and a lot of hours," Miriam said.

"The weird part is that Stephanie's mom asked my mom if she could give Stephanie rides to and from The Haven so she can still make her house showing appointments. She's going to pay my mom to help cover gas," Karen said.

"I bet Steph pushed to go to The Haven so she could see Flufftail," Anna said as she pulled her hair back in a ponytail. She always did that at lunch so her hair wouldn't get into her food.

"I bet you're right," Miriam said. "Is that squirrel still there, Karen?"

"I'm not sure, but I'll ask my mom," Karen said. "Sometimes, I feel a little bad for Stephanie. It really seems like she never sees her parents."

"Really? Do you remember how she cut the hole in the back of your gym shorts in fourth grade?" Michelle asked. "And how she put up those posters with caricatures of us after she made the fifth-grade cheer squad?"

"Okay — you're right. I did say 'sometimes,' and it would probably be just a little bit."

The bell rang and they all stood up to throw away their trash and head back to class.

"See you at Kindness Club after school," Grace said as they all went their separate ways. Kindness — now that's something Steph needs to learn, Miriam thought.

"Everyone will participate in the STEAM fair, but the grade requirements are pretty basic, as you can see on your handout. Everyone will create a poster that incorporates at least three parts of STEAM — science, technology, engineering, art, and math," Mr. Richardson said. He was Miriam's homeroom and math teacher. "There is a list of the topics we have covered so far this year to help inspire you. At least one topic must be covered on your poster. The school has received a donation for the fair this year, and we will provide you each with the poster board. The fair is not until the second-to-last week of March, but we wanted to give you the instructions now so you can think over winter break about what you might want to do. When we come back, I want you to have at least five ideas that we can start thinking over. Any questions?"

"Will we have to make a presentation?" a girl named Kristi asked. She was one of the top students in the seventh grade.

"You will make a presentation to the class as part of your grade, then your posters will be displayed in the gym for the competition, and the judges will base their decisions on what they see. You are allowed to have props and hands-on displays with your poster for the competition, but your grade will only depend on the poster and your class presentation. We want the fair to be a fun and friendly competition, but not part of your grade. Let's brainstorm some ideas."

Miriam's mind drifted off at that point. She already knew what she was going to do. It had come to her in the dream after she visited the island. Now that she finally had all the requirements, she would talk with Grandma about the specifics. She needed to start her project during Christmas break for it to be ready by March. She smiled as she doodled her idea on her handout.

She felt someone nudge her arm after a few minutes and looked up to see Michelle trying to get her attention. Mr. Richardson was now writing the math problems on the board that they needed to write down for homework.

"Thank you," she mouthed to Michelle and started writing the problems in her notebook, still smiling. She was sure her project was going to win the STEAM fair.

Grandma loved her idea.

"I want to build a self-sufficient aquaponic tank where the fish provide the nutrients for the plants to grow, and the plants provide the nutrients for the fish. Then, to incorporate art, I'll make a sun catcher to decorate the tank. We learned about fish ecosystems, so that covers something we learned about."

Since Christmas was only four days after break started and they were hosting Christmas dinner for a few of Grandma's friends, Grandma asked if they could wait to set it up until after Christmas. That was fine with Miriam.

"Plus, I invited the Mitchells over for Christmas dinner. Jeremy used to raise carp to sell, so I bet he would know a lot about how to set up the tank. His wife, Erin, is a master gardener with me, and the two of us could help you figure out the best plants to grow."

"That's even better! I really think I'm going to win first place with this idea!"

"Don't get your hopes up too quickly — focus on having fun with this and not on winning. I know Stephanie next door has an uncle who works for NASA. I wonder what she'll do for this project."

Miriam didn't want to think about Stephanie getting help from a NASA scientist. She just wanted to focus on her idea.

"Can you not tell anyone my idea except for the Mitchells? I don't want anyone to steal it."

"Don't worry, Miriam," Grandma told her. "I'll keep your idea close, but remember, it is just a seventh-grade assignment, not a competition for the Nobel Peace Prize."

True, Miriam thought to herself, but the look on Steph's face when she loses is going to be worth a Nobel Peace Prize.

Mr. and Mrs. Mitchell gave Miriam and her grandma lots of good advice and ideas at the Christmas dinner. They worked together over the next week, putting the tank together and starting some plants from seed to transplant to the tank. They took Sydney with them to go buy the carp since she was going to spend the night with Miriam the last Friday of winter break, which happened to be New Year's Eve. The tank would only fit two carp, so they picked a small orange and white one and a larger black and white one.

The girls each held one on the drive home. The carp had to stay in their bags in the tank water for 24 hours before releasing them from the bags.

"What are you going to name them?" Sydney asked.

"I've actually been thinking about that. I wanted to see them beforehand to make sure the names fit, but what do you think about Blue and Ribbon?"

"Umm, well, that might be unusual..."

"I'm just kidding! I was actually going to name them Beauty and Beast."

Sydney started laughing.

"You have to tell the other girls just like that! Michelle will love the Disney names, and Karen loves Beauty and the Beast as much as you do."

Miriam caught her grandma's eye in the rearview mirror and saw her wink. The names Blue and Ribbon had actually been Grandma's joke first. She had said, "With names like that, the judges would already think you should have first place."

After they got home and got the fish settled into the tank, they made homemade pizzas and started a *Star Wars* movie marathon. Grandma went to bed around 10 p.m. and told them to go to sleep right after midnight. They switched to the news around 11:30 p.m. so they could watch the ball drop in Times Square. It would be Miriam's first time to watch it live. When she lived with her aunt and uncle, they always put her to bed around 9 p.m. after watching a recording of the previous year's ball drop. Sydney said she had been staying up until midnight since she was seven for New Year's Eve.

"Do you have any New Year's resolutions?" Sydney asked during a commercial break.

"I do. I wrote them out yesterday. Do you?"

"Yes — I did the same thing! I am going to read 26 books this year, save 100 dollars and try out for the eighth-grade show choir. What are yours?"

"I put down trying out for the eighth-grade show choir, too! I also want to win the STEAM fair and start piano lessons again. I want to be able to play the pieces we sing for choir to practice better."

"I bet we both make show choir. We should start practicing together. I hear you not only have to sing for the tryout, but have to choreograph a two-minute dance to a song."

"Good idea. Oh, look, they're starting the countdown."

As the girls watched the countdown and the ball drop, Miriam was smiling. It was great to know she could use her yearly wish to help her achieve her resolutions. She felt she could accomplish anything. It was nice to finally have something work in her favor after losing her parents. They would want her to have a good life.

"Happy New Year!" Sydney said as she hugged Miriam, snapping her out of her train of thought.

"Happy New Year, Sydney! It's going to be a great year!"

Miriam only saw Stephanie on the bus, in choir, and during her special activity class. The first quarter was art, and the second quarter had been life skills, where they had learned to cook biscuits, sew on a button, and balance a checkbook. They never had to speak to each other during those classes, but every once in a while, Miriam would look up to find Stephanie staring at her. After winter break, they were going to the library where they would learn research and note-taking skills. The librarian paired them up in groups of four on the first day, and Miriam and Stephanie were together with two boys who were football players. Miriam just knew their names — Mark and Jeff — but had never really talked to them. Stephanie knew them already, though. She was talking to them about the football schedule until the librarian started talking. The three of them mostly ignored Miriam.

"On Mondays and Tuesdays, you will do research on a topic I will give you for the week. Each group will have a different topic. On Wednesdays and Thursdays, you will take notes and organize them to present to another group on Friday," Ms. Pinkerton said. "The first two weeks, I will be showing you all the available resources that you will be able to pull from. Today we're going to start with the Dewey Decimal system, so you know how to find books on the right shelves."

During those first two weeks, Ms. Pinkerton just gave them mini-lectures and tours around the library. They had to take notes, and there was a quiz they had to pass before they would be allowed to research. Miriam didn't have to talk to Steph until the Monday when they got their first research assignment.

There was an envelope at each table. The librarian told them to open it up and work together first to brainstorm what and how they wanted to research the topic. Steph snatched it up right away when Ms. Pinkerton was done talking.

"We have the Bermuda Triangle," Steph announced, looking Miriam square in the eye.

"Cool!" Mark said. "I watched a video about that with my parents last year. My older brother was researching it for a paper in college."

"What is it?" Jeff asked.

"It is a place in the ocean where ships and planes just disappear. The area is surrounded by three islands that give it the shape of a triangle. It even messed up Christopher Columbus' compass when he sailed over it," Mark told Jeff.

"So, where should we focus our research?" Miriam asked Mark.

"Yes, Mark, you should take the lead this week since you know so much about it already," Steph said as she smiled warmly at Mark.

Mark told them they should look at books on the topic, but to also look at Caribbean explorers and World War II missing aircraft. He mentioned looking at National Geographic for the video they had done on the topic and in their magazines. Mark and Steph would look through the books, and Miriam and Jeff would look at what National Geographic offered. As they were about to start looking, the bell rang.

"I'll ask my uncle tonight, too," Miriam heard Steph tell Mark as they were packing up their book bags. "He's helping me with my STEAM project. We're building a drone that can take aerial photographs. He works at NASA but is helping with some research in Kansas City for a few months with a government company."

"That's neat! Good idea to see if he knows any good resources," Mark said.

Miriam and Jeff just looked at each other, and Jeff rolled his eyes. The flirtation by Steph was obvious. Steph and Mark didn't even acknowledge Miriam or Jeff as they left the library together.

"Guess I'm not the cool one," Jeff said.

"Me neither," Miriam replied.

"See you tomorrow," Jeff said and walked out the library door.

Miriam walked slowly to her next class, thinking about what Steph said about her STEAM project. Her aquaponic tank was going well — the plants were starting to grow and were right on track to be blooming or producing crops by the time of the fair in two months. Beauty and Beast were very active and seemed to be happy in their environment. She was going to start working on her sun catcher next week. She had decided last night, after talking it over with Grandma, to make a design of the Earth.

I bet the judges will know Steph had help, Miriam thought. *What seventh-grader could build a drone that takes pictures all by herself?* Still, Miriam felt that wasn't enough to guarantee she would win, and Steph wouldn't.

She got to math class and sat down. The teacher announced a pop quiz, and Miriam had to stop thinking about Steph's project for a while.

"How is your STEAM project going?" Karen asked Anna at lunch later that week. They had all chosen very different areas, but Miriam was the only one who was focusing on winning at the fair. However, she didn't let her friends know she was sure of winning. The other girls were focusing on a good grade for their posters and presentation. Anna was growing three tomato plants in a quiet room and three tomato plants in a room that played music all the time. She had also created a system that would self-water the plants.

"The music plants are already a few days ahead of the quiet plants," Anna announced. "They have blossoms on them!"

"Who would have thought?" Michelle said. "I have to keep working on the code for my robot. He keeps turning left when I want him to turn right. I'm going to try and have him draw a picture, but I need to have him move in the right direction first."

"Miriam's fish are loving their tank," Sydney said. "I saw them over the weekend. I'm still working on writing the music to program into my keyboard. I keep humming lines from songs and trying to put them in. I have to make sure the music is original."

Karen was trying to design a computer program that would take a picture and turn it into abstract art. Grace was designing a habitat for humans to live in on Mars.

"I heard this week what Steph is doing with her NASA uncle," Miriam said. "She's making a drone that can take pictures. I'm sure she has him doing all the work."

"I know they have kits for drones, but you have to buy a pre-built one to have a camera on it," Grace said. "I wonder if she's just buying one and saying they built it."

"We'll know when we look at it," Sydney remarked.

"That's what I thought," Miriam agreed. "I'm sure the judges would be able to tell if someone had too much outside help on the project. If hers looks too professional, I don't think she'd have a chance at winning."

The girls kept talking about their projects and offering advice until the lunch bell rang. Miriam was still trying to think of something else she could do to ensure Steph didn't beat her at the fair. Maybe a loose wire would prevent it from flying? She didn't like the thought of being mean, but she had to make sure Steph didn't win. She didn't want Steph to be able to rub their noses in it for months, especially since she probably wasn't even lifting hardly a finger to work on it.

In library, their first few presentations went well, with Steph and Mark talking about what they had learned and Miriam and Jeff talking about what they found. Steph only talked to Miriam when it was absolutely necessary. However, just a few weeks before the STEAM fair, they got the topic of the 10 most recent animals added to the endangered species list. Just as they were about to split up into their own smaller groups, Miriam heard Steph talk about Flufftail.

'Mark, I rescued a baby squirrel once," she said.

"Really?"

"Its mother abandoned it by a tree in my backyard, and I took care of it for a full day. Then it was having trouble breathing, so I called The Haven just across the border in Kansas, and they came and took it to help it. I go visit him once a week to take care of him. I named him Flufftail," she said. She looked at Miriam, daring her to say something to correct her. Miriam almost stayed quiet, but then she remembered how Steph had tried to ruin Sydney's Halloween party.

"Don't forget to tell him about you bringing him to my house to ask for help and that you visit The Haven because you had to do community service after throwing a party at your house," Miriam reminded her. "You never visited Flufftail until you had to."

"That's not true. I wanted to, but my parents would never take me," Steph said. "And, I didn't really need your help that first night. I would have found The Haven on my own, but I thought your friends might need a distraction from being at your house."

Steph walked away before Miriam could say anything else. The boys just quietly looked at each other. Miriam walked to the other side of the library where she and Jeff did their research. She glanced back and saw Jeff heading towards her and Mark heading towards Steph.

"So, do you want to talk about what just happened, or do you want me to pretend I didn't see and hear that?" Jeff asked.

"She's just so mean and rude sometimes. She lives next door to me," Miriam looked up at Jeff. She barely knew him, and she really didn't feel like dragging a stranger into her little bit of Steph drama. "Never mind. You can pretend you didn't hear that. Let's find those endangered animals."

The librarian decided to give them the week off before the STEAM fair so they could do any last-minute work they needed to do on their projects.

"What if we're all done with our project?" Steph asked after Ms. Pinkerton made the announcement.

"You can read, do homework, write a letter — anything — as long as you're quiet and let the other students work," Ms. Pinkerton said.

Miriam was pretty much done with her poster, so she decided to put out some of the vegetables she'd grown in the tank on a plate for tasting. She had outlined her presentation, which included pictures of the tank and the plant growth along the way. Her earth sun catcher was done and looked really nice on the tank. She decided to use the time to research other aquaponic tanks to have some extra details for her presentation and maybe add to the poster for the judges.

Miriam had to walk through the fiction section to get to the non-fiction section, and she ran into Steph at the end of the aisle. Steph was holding a stack of six books, and they all fell to the floor. Miriam instinctively reached down to help Steph pick them up. She saw *Julie of the Wolves, Island of the Blue Dolphin, Hatchet,* and *A Wrinkle in Time* in the pile. Miriam was surprised Steph would enjoy classic books like that. Not that she had thought about it much, but she had guessed Steph would read light books or graphic novels. Miriam had just finished reading *Island of the Blue Dolphin* and was about to tell Steph it was a good book, but when she saw how Steph was glaring at her, she decided to keep quiet.

"Sorry," Miriam whispered as she handed her the last book. Steph didn't say a word and just walked back to the tables.

They staggered the students' presentations to the class throughout the week. They only had to bring their posters — all other display items would be brought in on Friday morning to set up in the gym. Miriam and Grandma had already recruited Sydney and her mother to help bring the aquaponic tank into school. They had a minivan with removable seats, so Miriam could drain about half of the water away and save it to be added back in at school. She had a plastic storage tub that she had cut half of the top off to put under the tank, just to make sure no water spilled in the van. Miriam and Sydney would sit next to the tank and hold it steady. Miriam was glad Grandma had convinced her to get a smaller tank than she originally wanted. While the two-foot tank limited her with the number of fish and plants, it was much easier to transport. They had figured out all the details Sunday night when the Harringtons came over for dinner. Grandma liked to thank people by feeding them. Both the girls gave practice presentations after dinner. Sydney had asked their teacher if she could record and play her song when she gave her presentation, saying it was hard to "hear" a poster. Sydney's homeroom teacher said she could, so she created an mp3 file and emailed it to him. Sydney's poster showed her original music and pictures of her programming the music on the computer. She also put pictures of tulips all over the poster, explaining that her seeing photos of the tulip fields in Holland in a magazine inspired the music. Miriam's poster went over the steps on how to build an aquaponic tank — from choosing the right size, to sterilizing the tank, to selecting the right fish, testing the water's pH levels, and choosing what plants to grow. Her last picture was of the food she was able to grow in the tank. One corner also had a drawing of her Earth sun catcher. Miriam's grandma and Sydney's parents asked them a few questions and then started talking about the latest city council news.

"Guess they're done with us," Sydney said to Miriam.

"Want to go get another piece of cake?"

"Sure," Sydney said.

"Are you nervous at all about your presentation?" Miriam asked as she cut a slice of German chocolate cake for herself and Sydney.

"A little. I've written some songs before but never really played them for anyone but family. I hope the class likes the music," Sydney said.

"I'm sure they will. It's a really neat song. I like the techno/reggae feel in the middle," Miriam assured her. "I'm ready for the presentation, but I'm more nervous about transporting the tank and what the judges will say."

"I'm sure we'll all get some kind of certificate or ribbon. I'm guessing one of the computer club guys will win. I think a few of them are building robots — and all by themselves — not with help from a NASA uncle."

Miriam stayed quiet. She wanted to win but didn't want her friends to know how badly she was focused on it. She didn't think they would understand why a win would mean so much to her.

Sydney's parents came into the kitchen just then and said it was time to go home.

"That cake was good, wasn't it?" Sydney's mom asked. "I always get spoiled when we eat with Mrs. Rodgers. Thank you very much. I'll come by around 7:30 in the morning on Friday, ready to transport Beauty and Beast."

"Thank you, Mrs. Harrington," Miriam said as they all walked out the front door.

"Have time to help with dishes before bed?" Grandma asked Miriam.

"Yes, I do," she replied.

Karen and Grace both had their presentations on Monday. Anna did hers on Tuesday. Sydney and Michelle presented on Wednesday, and only Miriam gave hers on Thursday. As each of them came to lunch, glowing about how well their presentations went, Miriam got more and more nervous. Michelle was in her class, and her robot that drew a picture of a rose had amazed everyone. Mr. Richardson asked a few questions of each student, and Miriam could tell he was trying to gauge how much of the project the student had completed versus how much his or her parents might have done. Miriam wasn't worried about his questions, but some of the student questions were not as easy or nice.

When Thursday came, Miriam only ate three bites of toast for breakfast. There were only five students that needed to present that day, and she was the first one. Michelle came over to her desk before the bell rang and tried to give her a pep talk. It helped a little.

The bell rang, Mr. Richardson took attendance and then told Miriam it was her turn. She walked to the front and set up her poster.

As soon as she started talking, she felt at ease. She pictured herself back in her living room, talking to Grandma and Sydney's parents. Before she knew it, her presentation was over, and the class was clapping. She answered all of Mr. Richardson's questions and then got a couple of questions from the class about the fish, and how the food tasted. One girl told her it was a cool idea and that she was going to try it over the summer. As Miriam sat back down at her desk, she felt more confident about the STEAM fair the next day. Her project was really good and unique. There might be several robots and drones, but hers would be the only aquaponic tank. The look on Steph's face when Miriam got the blue ribbon would be priceless.

Sydney and Miriam were the last ones setting up in the gym on Friday morning for the STEAM fair. Sydney was only going to put up her poster since she didn't want to bring her laptop or keyboard into school. The school promised that there would be parents keeping an eye on the projects all day when the gym doors weren't locked, but Sydney didn't want to risk it. Miriam was almost done refilling the tank when the warning bell rang.

"You can go, Sydney. I'm almost done," Miriam said. "Can you tell Mr. Richardson I'll be there in just a few minutes?"

"Sure," Sydney said and headed out. Miriam's grandma and Sydney's mom had headed out right after they got the tank set up on the table. Grandma had a yoga/Pilates class at the gym she wanted to try out, and Mrs. Harrington always volunteered at the local homeless shelter on Friday, putting together weekend food kits.

As Miriam finished up putting the water back in the tank, she noticed Steph's drone was only a few displays down from her. There were three parents in the gym, but they were standing by the door talking, not looking in her direction at all. Miriam checked one last time to make sure her display looked good. The plastic wrap was secure over her plate of vegetables, and Beauty and Beast were happily swimming. She would have to walk by Steph's display to get out of the gym. Steph's presentation looked very professional. There were detailed instructions on how to fly the drone and a laptop set up to see the photos it took. Miriam put her backpack down and tied her shoe. It wasn't fair that Steph could get so much help from her uncle when Miriam had done all the work on her project herself. She saw a small red wire on the drone and reached up and pulled on it gently as she stood up. It came out of the drone at one end. Now the judging would be a little fairer. She smiled, but then a feeling of dread came over her.

"Oh, I didn't know any students were still in here," one of the parents said as Miriam walked out the gym doors.

"I was just finishing putting water in my aquaponic tank and making sure my fish were okay. I'm heading to class now," Miriam replied.

"Anyone else in there?"

"No, it was just me."

She heard them talk about how they needed to keep a careful eye on the doors now to make sure no other students came in.

"It would be terrible if someone worked really hard and their project got ruined — whether on accident or purpose," Miriam heard one of the moms say.

The judges would come between 10 a.m. and noon, and there would be a school assembly at 1 p.m. to announce the winners. From 1:30 to

3 p.m., students would be able to stand by their displays, and parents could come to see, or the students could look around at other projects. At 3 p.m., they could start tearing down their displays. Sydney's mom and Miriam's grandma were going to come at 3:30 p.m. after most people had left, to transport the tank back home.

"Ms. Pinkerton, can you please send Miriam Stanley to the gym, please?" a voice came over the loudspeaker in the library.

"She'll be on her way. Miriam, let me write you a hall pass. We only have 10 minutes left, so take your backpack in case you're there for a while. Maybe the judge has a question for you."

Miriam wondered why they were calling her down. She hadn't heard anyone else get called to the gym, and they were told they wouldn't be interacting with the judges, so scores would only be based on their displays. What if one of the parents had seen her pull the wire on Steph's drone? That was probably it. How could she explain to Grandma why she had done such a thing? She hadn't felt good all day and wished she hadn't done it. She should have just trusted in her wish.

The gym doors were closed, and some different parents were standing outside. It was just a little after 10 a.m., so the judges should have just started judging.

"I got called to come to the gym," she told the one dad in the group.

"Are you Miriam?"

"Yes," she replied. "Why do they need me?"

"There's a problem with your tank — it's leaking. We want to know what you want us to do about the fish."

He opened the gym door, and Miriam pushed past him and ran to her display. The custodian was mopping up the floor, and there was duct tape in three places on her tank.

"What happened?" Miriam asked. There was less than half of the water left in the tank.

"No one knows, but they're investigating now. There are cameras everywhere around the building," the custodian said. "When the judges came in, they started in this row, and one noticed water on the floor. Be glad they started here, so it was found before all the water drained out."

A man in a suit came over to Miriam.

"I'm Mr. Jensen, and I'm one of the judges. I hope it's okay that we put some tape to cover up the leaks. We wanted to know if you just wanted to add water back in the tank or if the fish needed to go somewhere else," he said.

"The water is at a specific pH level. We should bag each fish separately in the water that is left. They can stay in the tank that way until I take them home," Miriam told him.

"There are plastic bags in the teacher's lounge," the custodian said. "I can go grab some. I think I got all the water up."

"Thank you," Miriam said.

Mr. Jensen helped Miriam bag up Beauty and Beast after the custodian brought back the bags. He made a few comments about how original her display was and patted her shoulder when they were done.

"I was told to ask you to visit the principal when we were done taking care of the fish," Mr. Jensen told her.

"Oh, okay," Miriam said.

"I think they now know how your tank had some leaks. Some kids came in the back door and messed with some displays. We're taking that into account with our judging," he said. Then he walked back over to the other judges, and they got back to work.

Miriam headed to the principal's office.

Steph, two other girls, and three boys were all sitting in chairs in the office waiting area. Right after Miriam walked in, the secretary said Mrs. Traine would see them now. All seven of them squeezed into the principal's office.

"You all know by now that your STEAM fair projects were damaged, and you have had the chance to fix them. I'm sorry some of you waited a while, but we wanted to take you to the gym one by one to keep an eye on everyone, and the judges needed to start the judging process. You will each be interviewed by the judges when I'm done talking with you so they can take that into account as part of your score since your displays were damaged. Luckily, the only project with live animals was Miriam's, and the fish are going to be just fine, right?"

"Yes, Beauty and Beast are doing fine. There was just enough water left in the tank," Miriam replied.

"The two students were caught on cameras by the back door of the gym. One of them had propped it open this morning when everyone was bringing their projects in. Those students hadn't completed their projects and wanted to ruin what they thought were the best ones. They are each suspended for seven days — one for each project. I am very sorry that this happened, but we are doing our best to make it as fair as possible for everyone despite this happening. Any questions?"

"What about the cost of the parts on my robot they broke? I saved up for weeks to buy those," the tallest boy asked.

"Your parents can call me to make an appointment to make a claim for monetary compensation for damages. Again, I apologize for all this," Mrs. Traine said. No one else spoke up, so Mrs. Traine told the students to report to the gym for their interviews after lunch. She told them they were excused from their classes for the rest of the day, so they could stay in the gym until the judging announcements. The lunch bell rang as they were leaving the office.

Miriam didn't talk much at lunch, even though her friends asked her how the fish were doing. Word had spread quickly about the damaged projects. Miriam gave them the few details she knew, and then they started guessing who might have done it. The talk turned to Steph's project being damaged, too, and Miriam began to feel sick to her stomach.

"I'm going to head out and check on the fish again," Miriam announced. She hadn't eaten a bite of her lunch.

"I'll go with you," Sydney said. She was up before Miriam could object. Miriam had been thinking of going to the principal to confess what she did, but she couldn't do that with Sydney with her. They went to the gym, and Miriam showed Sydney the bags with the fish in them.

"They really cracked the tank on purpose? That's just awful. I'm glad they left your suncatcher alone. It's so pretty," Sydney said. "At least they're letting you guys talk to the judges. It's hard to evaluate a project when it's damaged."

"They left my vegetable samples alone, too," Miriam said. "I guess trouble makers don't like vegetables."

Just then, Steph walked into the gym. She walked right past Miriam and Sydney without saying a word or even glancing at them. The warning bell rang, and Sydney left to go to class. Miriam adjusted her poster a bit and watched Steph out of the corner of her eye. She picked up her drone and examined it all over, making sure each wire was tight and in the right place. She grabbed the remote and flew the drone for a few seconds, making it go up, down, right, and left. She then checked the photo feed on the laptop. It really looked like Steph knew what she was doing, which surprised Miriam. Maybe Steph had done some of her own work on her project. Maybe Miriam didn't really need to say anything about what she did — it would all work out all right. Her desire to beat Steph had pretty much faded away, though. She should never have touched Steph's project. Deep down, she was pretty sure she had negated the effects of her wish. She was supposed to do the work, and the wish would come true. Sabotaging someone else was not doing the work. It really was cheating.

The same judge from this morning tapped her on the shoulder and asked if she was ready for her interview. She took a deep breath and smiled. She would tell them all about her aquaponic tank and let the results fall where they may.

Miriam sat with her friends during the assembly. Results were announced by grade level, starting with the seniors and working their way down. Mrs. Traine talked for several minutes at the beginning about how proud they were and how the school planned to make it an annual event. Not one word was spoken about the damaged projects, probably because there were lots of parents standing around the walls of the gym to hear the results, too. A local newspaper was there to cover the results as well.

Miriam couldn't focus very well on the other grades' results. She was nervous. She kind of wanted to win, but she also just wanted to fade into the background and move on so she didn't have to think about what she did to Steph.

"In third place is Steven Landers with his transforming robot. In second place is Stephanie Risner with her photographing drone. And, our first place project for the seventh grade is Miriam Stanley with her aquaponic tank."

"You won!" Sydney cried.

"Go, Miriam," Karen said as she hugged her.

Steven, Steph, and Miriam all walked up front to get their certificates and have their photo taken. Miriam didn't feel as happy as she thought she would, but she smiled for the picture.

"Congrats, Steph," Miriam said as they walked back to the bleachers.

"I don't know why you got first. Your project didn't even involve any technology," Steph said and then walked away. Mrs. Traine was dismissing the students to go stand by their projects and asking the parents to wait just a few minutes before walking around to look at them. After 30 minutes, she would release the students to go look around at other projects, too. If students left before 3 p.m., they needed to be signed out at the office.

Miriam's friends were so excited for her, and each one gave her a hug or high five. Then they all walked to their project displays.

Miriam knew her grandma was not going to show up for a while, but she had several parents stop by and ask her about her project. A few said they wanted to try it at home. She decided to stay by her display when the students walked around so she could keep an eye on Beauty and Beast. She'd have to ask Grandma if they could go buy a new tank tonight. She would make sure to remember to tell Grandma she could make a claim with the school for the cost. Most of the students were gone by the time Miriam's grandma and Sydney's mom came. Steph was still there, and her parents had just shown up, too.

"You missed the awards ceremony. I won second place," Miriam heard Steph say.

"You didn't win first?" her dad asked. "After we flew your uncle out for the day, you were supposed to win first place." Her dad's phone rang, and he took the call.

Steph's mom was texting on her phone and looked up when her husband's phone rang.

"Really? You were supposed to take her home. I have three showings tonight — all in the half-million-dollar range," she said.

"It's an emergency," he replied as he ended the call. "And my client lives in a million-dollar house. Just take her home before your showing."

Miriam looked at her grandmother, who had heard the whole exchange, too. Grandma walked over to Steph's parents and offered to take Steph home. They accepted and left the gym, not even saying goodbye to their daughter. Miriam couldn't help feeling sorry for Steph. Her parents didn't even look at her project at all. The girls stayed quiet on the drive home while the adults talked about spring break plans. Steph did thank Mrs. Harrington when she left the van to walk up her sidewalk. Miriam realized Steph was probably pretty lonely.

"Grandma, I did something wrong, and I'm not sure what to do about it," Miriam said as they sat down to eat dinner. Grandma had made bacon cheeseburgers and French fries to celebrate. It was Miriam's favorite meal, but she didn't have any appetite.

"What did you do?" Grandma asked as she sat down across from Miriam.

"One of the projects today wasn't damaged by the two boys. It was damaged by me," Miriam confessed. She couldn't look her grandmother in the eye.

"If you accidentally damaged a project, I'm sure you could just talk to the person, and they would understand," Grandma said.

"No, Grandma, I did it on purpose."

"Tell me. It's okay."

"I wanted to win the STEAM fair so badly, I even made it my wish. But I wasn't sure I would win after I saw Steph's poster and drone. I didn't think it was fair that she got help from her uncle that works for NASA, and the rest of us had to work on our own. So, I pulled a wire from her drone when I was done setting up the fish tank."

Miriam looked up at her and expected to see anger in her eyes. Instead, she saw concern.

"I wish I hadn't done it, Grandma. I saw Steph fix her drone — she knew what she was doing. Then, her parents didn't even spend more than a minute with her and only complained that she didn't get first. I don't deserve first place," Miriam started crying softly.

"I'm glad you told me, Miriam," she said and put her hand on Miriam's arm. "You could have just kept quiet, but the way you're talking, I think that would eat at your soul. I do have an idea about how you can make this right."

On Monday morning, Miriam and her grandma went and talked to the principal. She agreed to their idea, even though she still would have to suspend Miriam for one day and take a day off the other boys' suspension. Since Miriam confessed, the principal was willing to not give out all the details to the school. Mrs. Traine would call Stephanie, Steven, and the fourth-place winner, Adam Lee, down to her office and tell them that the judges made a miscalculation and had discovered it as they were reviewing their sheets over the weekend. Stephanie had actually won first place, and Miriam had placed fourth. She would then call all their parents to inform them of the mistake and ask the newspaper to come and take a new photo.

"Since this is your first offense and you confessed on your own, I will just make a note in your file with the one-day suspension," Mrs. Traine said. "However, Miriam, I want you to understand this is serious, and if you do anything like this again, the punishment will be severe."

"I understand," Miriam told her. "Thank you."

"See you tomorrow."

Miriam decided not to tell her friends what she did to Steph. Her friends all told her they felt terrible that the judges had changed their minds and that she was first place in their minds. She definitely felt like she didn't know Steph very well and felt sorry for her not really being able to see her parents a lot. It must be lonely. When her friends brought up Steph, she tried to change the conversation. She was starting to think that Steph needed a second chance, but she wasn't sure how to go about it. She had started doing one thing nice toward Steph — she chose her as her target for the Kindness Club. Every Monday and Friday, she snuck an encouraging note in Steph's locker. Just once, she caught Steph finding the note and smiling.

Chapter 7

It was the last week of school when Miriam got an idea to find a way for Steph to start hanging out with her friends more. The librarian had given each homeroom teacher a list of recommended books to read over the summer. They were required to read three and turn in book reports during the first week of school. The list had about 50 different titles on it, but they could choose any book. The only requirements were that the book had to be more than 100 pages and not a graphic novel. Miriam looked at the list and saw almost all of the books Steph had dropped in the library. *We should have a summer book club*, Miriam thought. *I bet Steph could get permission to come next door for a book club, especially if Grandma talked to Steph's mom about it.*

Miriam told her friends about the plan during the last week of school. She had designed a flyer and showed it to them at lunch.

"I'm going to have a summer book club," Miriam said as she handed each a flyer. "I picked three of the books from the summer reading list, and we can meet and talk about them."

"That's a great idea!" Sydney agreed. "I may have to miss July's meeting since we're going to Washington, D.C., around that time."

"I can make that one, but I'll be out of town for June," Karen said.

"I'm going to pass them out to most of the seventh graders we know," Miriam told them. "I think there may be some people that love to read but probably don't show it at school."

"We can help you pass them out," Anna offered.

"That's great that your grandma is letting you have this at your house," Michelle said.

"If it gets too big, she said we could move it to the library since it's only three blocks away, but I'm hoping the weather will be nice and we can have it in the backyard," Miriam said.

"I'm not looking forward to having to read so much over summer," Grace said, "but this will make it a little bit fun to be able to talk about the books. Have you read these ones yet?"

"I've read *Island of the Blue Dolphins*, but not *White Fang* or *The Diary of Anne Frank*," Miriam said.

Karen had read them all, but no one was surprised at that. She said they were excellent choices.

Miriam debated telling them she planned to invite Steph but decided against it. She didn't want them to plan to do anything to her. She was hoping that if Steph just showed up and they all talked about books, they could all start getting along better.

Her friends had started talking about the math final. However, Miriam was thinking about her talk with Grandma last night about taking the flyer over to Steph's. Grandma said she would watch for a time when Mrs. Risner was home and go over there to offer to watch Steph on book club days. Miriam felt confident her plan would work.

For the June book club, Sydney came over a few hours early to help Miriam make brownies and lemonade. When the doorbell rang, Grandma got up to get it.

"Hi, Stephanie. So glad you could make it. Your mom called and said you could stay until she got home tonight around six."

"Thanks, Mrs. Rodgers. Mom said I could decide whether to come or not, but our Internet is out, so I guess this would be better."

"Steph is coming to book club?" Sydney whispered to Miriam.

"Guess so," Miriam replied and tried to shrug innocently.

"Miriam and Sydney are in the kitchen making brownies if you want to join them," Grandma told her. "Or you can wait in the backyard where the book club will meet."

Steph came in and peeked in the kitchen at Miriam and Sydney.

"Hi, Steph. You can come help us if you want," Miriam said.

"Okay," Steph replied and slowly walked into the kitchen. Her entire demeanor was different than when she was at school with her cheerleader friends. She seemed quieter and more subdued.

"How's your squirrel?" Miriam asked.

"Flufftail is fine. Mr. Jensen at The Haven has been teaching him some tricks. They plan to take him along when they do presentations to raise more money for The Haven," Steph replied.

"That's pretty neat," Sydney said. "Remember when they brought the shelter dogs to school in fourth grade, and they did tricks for an assembly?"

"Yes — my favorite was the little dog that would sit on the big dog's back as the big dog walked around the stage," Steph said.

Miriam was surprised at how easy Sydney and Steph were talking to each other.

"Time to taste-test the batter," Miriam announced. They all took a spoonful of brownie batter and declared it good. Miriam put the brownies in the oven.

"Can you girls help me put chairs up in the backyard? We have several yard chairs in the garage," Miriam asked.

As they set up the chairs, Miriam's other friends and about ten more seventh graders started showing up. Most of the parents knew Grandma from one activity or another, but a few stopped at the door to talk to her before letting his or her kid stay for book club. Miriam was busy welcoming people as they arrived and setting up the snacks on a table in the backyard, but she noticed her friends grouped together and whispering. She wanted to see what they were talking about, but the doorbell rang again. She went to answer it and hoped her friends were just chatting about everyday things and not Steph.

After Miriam got the last guest settled, it was time to start the book club. She hadn't gotten to talk to her friends yet.

To Miriam's relief, the book club discussion went really well with everyone participating, including Steph. Her friends interacted with Steph as nicely as they did with the other students there. Steph left as soon as the discussion was over, despite Grandma asking her to stay for a while. Steph mumbled something about a movie and headed back to her house.

Miriam's friends were staying to eat dinner after the book club. They all talked about how surprised they were that Steph actually came over.

"I saw that she was reading this book back when we were in the library together," Miriam told them. "I was surprised she was reading books like this, but I guess today proves she actually read *Island of the Blue Dolphins,* at least. Did you guys know she was a reader?"

"She would bring a book when we went to the pool in the summer to read during lifeguard breaks, but I never saw her read much anywhere else," Sydney said.

"Maybe she hides it because reading doesn't fit in with the cheerleader persona," Karen said.

"So, I know she hasn't been the friendliest to us, but what if we try to ask her to join us for a few things this summer. Her parents are gone all day most days, and she's not allowed to leave the house or have anyone over when they're gone. My grandma can get permission from her mom for her to join us, though. You should have seen her parents at the end of the STEAM fair — they were so upset she got second place instead of first and fought over who had to take her home," Miriam said.

"I wouldn't mind giving her another chance, especially after today," Sydney said. "It is actually really sad. Steph's parents were great until her mom miscarried her baby brother and found out they couldn't have any more children. Then, they both threw themselves into their work, and Steph found cheerleading."

"I didn't know that," Miriam told her. "That is really sad."

"Let's ask her to join us to make the cupcakes for The Haven's fundraiser in two weeks when Karen is back," Anna suggested.

"Great idea!" Michelle agreed. "It would be nice to have Steph as a friend again."

Steph did come and make cupcakes with them and also came to the next book club. After that, she had permission to come over to Miriam's house anytime, but only there. Miriam finally saw the nice, friendly side of Steph that smiled. She came over at least twice a week just to hang out with Miriam. When she didn't show up the afternoon of the last book club, just two weeks before school started, Miriam was worried. She called, but no one answered. Sydney went over to knock on the door, but no one answered. Sydney was the last one to leave that afternoon, and as Miriam saw her out, they saw a car drive up to Steph's house. Her parents got out, and then Steph's dad opened the back door and started helping Steph out. Her leg was in a cast, and she had to use crutches. They both ran over to see what had happened.

"It was the first day of cheerleading practice this morning, and I fell off the pyramid and broke my leg," Steph told them. She was trying to hold back her tears, but a few were running down her cheeks. "The doctor said I won't be able to cheer until after Christmas."

"Oh, Steph, I'm so sorry," Sydney told her.

Miriam was watching Steph's parents. They had both pulled out their phones while Steph was talking to them.

"Steph, you have to come in now. I need to get you settled so I can make my evening showings," her mom said. "I'll see if Jenny can be on standby to come over in case your father gets called in."

"I don't need a babysitter," Steph said angrily.

"You'll need help getting food and getting upstairs to bed," her mom said. "No arguing with me."

Miriam leaned over and whispered to Steph that she would talk to Grandma. Both girls told Steph to call them if she needed anything or wanted to talk. Sydney started walking to her house, and Miriam went back to hers. She saw Steph struggling to use the crutches to get up the three steps to the front porch. Her mother was already inside, but her father was just watching Steph struggle. She went in quickly to talk to her grandma.

Steph practically lived with Miriam until school started back up. They even took her to eighth-grade orientation with them, a smaller version of the seventh-grade orientation. Even though Steph had her cheerleader shirt on, the other cheerleaders tended to ignore her. At that moment, Miriam was glad she had found a way for Steph to be friends with her friends again. Between her parents and the cheerleaders, Steph would be very lonely if she didn't have her old friends back. While Miriam missed her parents, she couldn't quite imagine the loneliness Steph must feel without her parents' love and attention when she was living with them.

After they compared schedules, they all convinced Steph to join them in The Kindness Club.

"I think I'm going to start up a book club this year," Steph told them. "I really enjoyed getting together to talk about books this summer. Would you guys join if I got it started?"

"Yes!" they all said together. Steph smiled and headed over to the Vice Principal to ask how she could start up a new club.

On the first day of school, Miriam met up with Sydney, Steph, and Anna for choir after homeroom. They all sat together the first day, knowing they would be split up into the alto and soprano sections within a few days.

"I have a fun announcement to make," Mrs. Troute said. "This year, the school is going to have a talent show instead of the STEAM Fair. They are going to alternate every other year to give students a chance to do both. I hope all of you consider sharing your musical talent. The tryouts will be at the end of January, and the show will be the week before spring break in March."

Miriam paid close attention to all the details of the talent show. She had just started thinking over the weekend about her next wish, and now she knew what she should wish for — she would work on a great solo and win fair and square this year. She would definitely ask Grandma about piano lessons tonight so she could get better at playing the music she wanted to sing.

"Did everyone hear about the talent show?" Anna asked at lunch. Karen hadn't had music class yet, so they told her about it.

"Maybe we could do something together," Karen suggested. "Like a funny skit or a dance routine?"

"I'm out for dancing," Steph said. She was still on crutches.

"Oh, sorry. I forgot," Karen replied.

"That's okay," Steph responded.

"We could sing a song," Sydney said. "The newest Angels song is pretty catchy."

"I was thinking of doing a solo actually," Miriam said.

"I don't think I could sing on stage," Michelle confessed. "I don't even like to raise my hand in class."

"I know — let's all bring ideas to Steph's birthday sleepover next month, and we can try them out," Sydney offered.

"Great idea," Karen said. "Hey, speaking of Angels, did you see Trina's dress at the awards show last night?"

At dinner that night, Miriam asked about taking piano lessons. Grandma said she would be fine paying for lessons as long as Miriam practiced every day.

"I think Mrs. Turner from Master Gardeners gives lessons, and she just lives two blocks away," Grandma told her. "I'll contact her tomorrow and see how much she charges. I know your parents loved having you in piano lessons."

"Thank you, Grandma." Miriam smiled.

"I tried to get your mother to take piano lessons when she was about your age, but she wouldn't have anything to do with it," Grandma said. "She just wanted to read all the time. Oh, I forgot to tell you, I got a long email from Aunt Susan and Uncle Mike. I printed it out for you. They're coming to visit next summer!"

"Really? For how long? Will they stay with us?" Miriam asked. She missed her aunt and uncle but tried not to think about them too much so she didn't get sad.

"They'll spend two weeks with us then go to Nebraska to spend some time with Mike's family. They have a month vacation time before they have to head back," Grandma replied.

Miriam went to read the email after dinner and started to feel bad for not staying in better touch with her aunt and uncle. They had two whole paragraphs just addressed to her with questions about school and how excited they were to come to see her. They missed her, but there was a girl in the orphanage who often reminded them of her because of her love for music. They said they prayed for her every day.

Miriam decided to make more of an effort to email them every weekend. She was glad she still had so many family members who loved her and cared for her. Every time she thought of how Steph barely saw her parents, she treasured her own family more.

"I'm going to email Aunt Susan and Uncle Mike back now if that's okay with you, Grandma."

"Sure, just finish up the dishes and your homework when you're done," Grandma said. "I have to make a few phone calls about the fundraiser for the Master Gardeners."

"Will do," Miriam replied.

Uncle Mark and Aunt Susan,

I am so glad I get to see you next summer! I am sorry I haven't written very much. I know Grandma keeps you posted on how busy I am with school and friends, but I do think of you guys often.

There's going to be a talent show in eighth grade this year, and I plan to start piano lessons back up. I want to play and sing for the talent show. My friends want to do an act together, so I have to see if I can do both.

Stephanie, the girl who lives next door, has become friends with us now. She joined our book club over the summer, then broke her leg and couldn't do cheer.

She joined us in Kindness Club and seems happier now. Her parents don't give her a lot of attention.

What is the name of the girl who reminds you of me? Can she email or write to me? It would be neat to have a pen pal from Kenya, especially one who loves music.

I will be better emailing you. I miss you guys, too, but I am doing well with Grandma. Thank you for the prayers! Hugs!

Love,

Miri

The fall passed by quickly for Miriam. School was a bit harder in eighth grade, so she spent more time on homework every night. She also tried to practice piano at least 30 minutes every day, but she often played for much longer. She still had Beauty and Beast to take care of, but she was no longer growing any plants in their tank. She did find out she could do both a group and a solo act for the talent show, but she didn't know if her friends would actually do a group number. They usually got together Friday nights at Sydney's house to practice, but it usually ended up being time for them to just hang out and chat.

They were still deciding between two songs by the time Miriam's birthday rolled around. She decided to forgo a sleepover that year, and instead, they celebrated her birthday at Sydney's on the Friday before her birthday. Her island visit would be on a Monday this year. She was really looking forward to it. She wanted to talk to Stella about how her wish ended up coming true, but then she had changed the outcome. When Sydney's mom found out they were going to celebrate Miriam's birthday, she insisted on having a cake, and Miriam's friends each got her a small, thoughtful present. Steph got her a beautiful hardback copy of *Island of the Blue Dolphins* and thanked her again for asking her to join the book club so she could be a friend to her friends again. They painted their nails, tried singing some songs for the talent show, and finally fell asleep at 3 a.m.

They woke up at 9 a.m. to the smell of bacon and pancakes. Miriam thought as she woke up that it had been one of the best birthday celebrations she had experienced since her parents had died. She couldn't wait to hear their voices again in a few days.

"Grandma, I'm nervous about going to the island tomorrow night," Miriam confessed at dinner Sunday night. "I wonder what the Volturians will think about what I did at the STEAM Fair. Do you think they'll be mad? Will they tell me I can't come anymore?"

"I don't think they can keep you from coming — you have to choose to go or stay," Grandma replied. "I think the fact that you're worried about it means that you'll be fine. You are sorry, and you fixed what you did."

"Would you consider my wish as having come true?" Miriam asked.

"Hmmm, that's hard to say. You did win like you wished to, but then you didn't win because you took matters into your own hands. Would you have won if you hadn't messed with Steph's drone? We'll never know. But you learned a lesson through it all, and maybe that's the point. Remember, your parents had a wish for you, and that had to come true, too."

"I do wonder what they wished for sometimes," Miriam said. "I honestly don't have a big wish this year, but I want to go to the island just so I can hear my parents' voices and make sure I find out what they wished for in the end."

"I hope you keep going every year, too," Grandma agreed. She kissed the top of Miriam's head as she cleared the dishes from the table. "I think your parents would be proud of the young lady you're becoming."

Grandma went to her room and came back to the table with a giant cupcake and a present.

"Happy birthday, Miribug. I got you something small this year, but I think you'll like it," she said. "Plus, the cupcake is strawberry cheesecake — your favorite."

"Thank you, Grandma," said Miriam. They split the cupcake and ate it first and then Miriam opened her present. It was a photo album with photos of her and her parents. Miriam looked through it without saying a word. Her heart ached and wished they were there with her as she turned 14.

Grandma came behind her and put her hands on Miriam's shoulders.

"This is one part of the present. I think you're old enough to treasure some things I saved for you. I put a box in your room with items from your parents that I saved for you to have. Each has a special story behind it and as you're ready, ask me what they are. This photo album was kept on your mom's nightstand. I know she would look through it often and worked hard to stay on top of adding new pictures in it as your family created memories."

Miriam closed the photo album and turned around to look at her. They both had tears in their eyes.

"Thank you, Grandma. I often wished I had more things to remind me of Mom and Dad. I'm glad you thought to save some of their things for me."

Miriam stood up and hugged her.

"I love you, Miribug."

"I love you, too."

Miriam hardly paid attention in any of her classes Monday. The clock seemed to move slowly, and she was waiting for the world to go dark. She practiced piano for a full hour after school and then started dinner since Grandma was trying a new class at the fitness center and wouldn't be home until dinnertime.

Grandma suggested they eat dinner while watching *Jeopardy* that night, something they rarely did — she knew Miriam could use a distraction. After the dishes were done, Miriam told her good night, even though it was still very early.

"Just make sure you get your homework done," Grandma said. "And enjoy your time on the island. I can't wait to hear about it tomorrow."

Miriam worked on her math and science homework in her room but looked up every few minutes to glance at the attic door or out the window at the street lamps. Nothing had lit up by the time she finished her homework, so she sat in her window seat and tried to read. Finally, after what seemed like an eternity to Miriam, the street lamps went on. She put the book down and stared, willing the lights to flicker. She didn't have to wait long. They flickered, and she looked toward the attic door — the words were glowing. It was time to go to Orphan Wish Island.

The warmth of an island breeze hit Miriam as soon as she opened the attic door. She stepped through the door and onto the island, feeling a wave of peace and happiness pass over her. She smiled as she walked over to the Starfruit tree. Only two others were standing there — Aaron and the girl with red hair. Miriam couldn't remember her name. Stella flew up just as Miriam got to the tree.

"One, two, three," Stella counted. She looked all around the perimeter of the island. "I was hoping everyone would show up this year, but I'm glad that you three are here. How was your year?"

"Great!" Aaron said. "I got on the basketball team and scored in every game. I practiced every day, and it paid off. I learned my lesson after the last year."

"Wonderful, Aaron!" Stella said.

"Mine ended up okay," the red-headed girl said. "We had to move in with my grandparents, so I had to start in a new school halfway through the year, but I did get a puppy and made some friends in the new neighborhood."

"What did you name the puppy?" Stella asked.

"Willow. She's a black lab," she replied.

"Wonderful name, Lexi," Stella said. Miriam made a mental note to remember the name.

"I ended up winning the STEAM Fair at school but made a huge mistake and gave up my blue ribbon," Miriam said quietly.

"Oh, yes, doing the right thing after doing something wrong is never easy, but it's the best way to live, Miriam," Stella said. "Shall we make this year's wishes? Do you all remember how to do it?"

"Yes," they said in unison and started looking for their name on the Starfruit. Miriam found hers rather quickly but walked about 10 feet away and sat down before taking a bite. She wanted to be ready to hear her parents' voices.

"We love you more than the world! Be good and be kind," her mom said.

"And be smart, Miribug," her dad said. "Bye."

Miriam wiped the tears from her cheeks and whispered her wish, "I want to be the best singer and piano player at the talent show. I don't have to win, but I want to be the best at what I do."

She stood up and found the spot where she had buried her other Starfruit. Small trees were beginning to sprout up. She buried her third Starfruit, and Stella flew over as she stood back up.

"I have two questions for you before I go home," Miriam said.

"I bet I can answer them," Stella replied with a smile.

"First, what happens to these trees from the fruit that we're planting?"

"That is an easy one. We use the trees for other future islands. The tree you're wishing from grew from an orphan's wish made 78 years ago. The magic is powerful but takes a long time to grow. The trees don't bear fruit until 50 years after they're planted, and names don't appear until they are 75 years old."

"Wow, so my wish will help others someday?" Miriam was astounded.

"Yes," Stella said. "Now, what is your second question?"

"Would you say my wish came true for last year or not? It came true because I won, but I won because I interfered, which means it didn't come true. Then, I had to give up being in first place to make things right. I just don't know what to think," Miriam admitted.

"I think a better question to ask would be if it matters if your wish came true exactly as you wished it or if you became a better person for what happened. In the end, does it matter if your wish came true or not? Or, does it matter that you did the right thing in the end?"

"I thought it wasn't polite to answer a question with a question," Miriam said. She was smiling, though, knowing Stella had asked her some good questions. It didn't matter if her wish came true or not as long as she did the right thing. That was what mattered.

"But sometimes it is best," Stella said. "Now, you go and enjoy the rest of your year."

"Thanks, Stella. You're a wonderful fairy."

"I'm NOT a fairy!" Stella yelled. They both laughed as Miriam walked toward her door. Aaron had already left, and Lexi was burying her fruit. As she turned to take one last look at the island before closing the attic door, she saw Amelia running toward the tree. One more wish would be made this year.

Miriam peeked to make sure Grandma had gone to bed already before she got settled into bed herself. She'd tell her all about the visit in the morning. She looked over at the picture of her parents and smiled. It was a wonderful gift to be able to hear their voices and receive a wish from them every year. Miriam fell asleep quickly, feeling happy and loved.

Chapter 8

Miriam and her friends were going to have another Halloween party but planned to be more selective about who was invited, mainly to control how many people showed up. Steph would be allowed to come if she got good enough grades on her first quarter report card. They had been helping her study math on the Friday nights they got together. They all gathered at her locker on the Wednesday before the party as report cards were handed out in the last class of the day.

"Did you open it yet?" Miriam asked Steph as she walked up to the group.

"No," Steph replied. "I'm worried. If I even get one 'B' my parents won't let me come on Friday. Here — open it for me."

She held the report card out. No one reached for it at first, so Sydney reached out for it. She opened it and looked over it with a straight face for a full minute before grinning.

"All A's!" Sydney cried. They all hugged Steph and started walking toward the bus area.

"I'm so glad you get to come to the party," Miriam told her as they got on the bus.

"Me, too," Steph agreed. "It'll be a great way to celebrate getting this cast off my leg on Friday!"

Miriam decided to check her email and send a quick note off to her aunt and uncle about her grades. She had gotten all A's, too. While there was more homework, she felt like she understood everything taught in her classes. Her math teacher suggested she test for the higher-level math class for her freshman year. She had been emailing her aunt and uncle every week this year, and it was great to feel closer to them again.

When she opened her email account on the computer, she had an email from GasiraO with the subject of "Hello from Kenya Pen Pal." Her aunt and uncle had told her a few weeks ago that they had found a few girls who might like a pen pal, but she hadn't heard any exact names. There were no attachments, and Miriam knew not to click on any links, so she opened the email to see what it said.

Miriam,

Mr. Mike and Ms. Susan gave me your email address to have a pen pal. I live in the orphanage but in a different building than your aunt and uncle. I have been here since I was a baby. My parents and older sister died of disease when I was six months old. They don't know why I survived. Only me and three other children in the village survived.

Ms. Susan teaches me English and home economics. I would love to see America one day, but I am working very hard right now to be accepted to the local public school. Mr. Mike thinks I will do very well on the tests. If I don't get in, I will go to the private school in town, but very few people get into university if they do not get into public school.

I like to draw, cook, and read. I often stay up too late at night reading. I am reading 'The Secret Garden' right now.

What do you like to do? What is your school like? What do you want to become?

I hope you write back soon!

Your Pen Pal,

Gasira Oteiro

Miriam was excited to have a pen pal from Kenya. She would have to tell Karen about it tomorrow. Karen had just finished reading about African fairy tales. Maybe she could set up other pen pals for her friends with children from the orphanage. Miriam decided to write Gasira back later that night or tomorrow. She needed to write to her aunt and uncle and then practice the piano. She had two tests tomorrow to study for, too — math and science.

Miriam practiced piano until dinner was ready, and then told her grandma about her new pen pal over dinner. Then, it was time to study. Miriam had barely read for 10 minutes after studying before she felt her eyes getting heavy. At this rate, eighth grade was going to pass by quickly.

Miriam wrote Gasira back as she was waiting to head over to Sydney's for the Halloween party. She was going as Pocahontas this year. She wondered what boys would show up to the party. Karen and Anna both had boyfriends this year, but they really just sat together at assemblies and football games. Miriam told Gasira about the Halloween party and asked if they celebrated that in Kenya. She told her about what she was reading and about the talent show coming up. She also told her she was sorry to hear about her family and told Gasira about her parents. She attached pictures of herself, Grandma, her friends, and Beauty and Beast, and asked for pictures of Gasira and her friends.

Miriam said goodbye to Grandma, grabbed her bag and sleeping bag, and headed to Steph's to help her with her bags. They were going to stay the night at Sydney's with Anna, Karen, Michelle, and Grace. They were heading over at 5 p.m. for pizza and to help Sydney with the decorations and food. The party would start at 7 p.m. and end at 10 p.m.

When Steph answered her door, Miriam could tell she had been crying.

"What's the matter?"

Steph just looked down at her leg. Miriam's eyes looked down, too, and she saw that there was a cast still on Steph's leg.

"You still have the cast! I thought you were getting that off today," Miriam cried.

"I have to wait two more weeks," Steph told her. "My dad was late picking me up from school, and by the time we got to the doctor, they couldn't see me anymore. The next appointment they had that my dad could take me to is in two weeks."

"I'm so sorry, Steph." Miriam hugged her. "It will come off, though. Here, let me get your bags for you."

"You're right. I just wish my dad had been on time. He got a call on the way back to school and decided it would be easier to just drop me off at home and then head into work."

"Well, you're going to have fun tonight," Miriam told her. "Do you have everything for your costume?"

"I do. You're right. Let's get to Sydney's so we can have some fun," Steph said.

Miriam told her friends all about her new pen pal while they ate pizza. They all thought it would be a great idea to be paired up with a pen pal in an orphanage.

"What if we did something for the orphanage through the Kindness Club? Like something for Christmas?" Karen suggested.

"That's a great idea!" Miriam said. "I'll email my aunt and uncle and see if they have any specific ideas, then bring them to our next meeting."

They spent the next two hours talking and decorating the basement. The party was fun. Miriam, Michelle, and Grace spent most of the time together talking or singing karaoke. Sydney was busy playing hostess, and Karen and Anna spent their time talking with the few boys who had shown up. They tried watching an old scary movie after the party ended but started giggling at all the scary parts because the music and special effects made it seem cheesy to them.

The next morning, Sydney asked them all if they really wanted to do a talent show act together or not.

"I'm not sure I want to get up on stage," Karen said. "Is it okay if I just help you with costumes and cheer you in the audience?"

"I'm not a fan of the stage, either," Michelle admitted.

"Do you know if we can do a group act and a solo act?" Anna asked. "If we can only do one, Miriam's out."

"Mrs. Ritzer said you could do one solo and one group act when I asked her," Miriam said.

"I would like to do something with you guys, but I'm not sure how well I'll be able to dance around," Steph said. "Hopefully, the cast will be off in two weeks, but I'll need physical therapy."

"What if we just sat and sang a song — me, Steph, Grace, and Anna?" Sydney asked. "Maybe Miriam could also be our accompanist."

"That sounds good to me," Miriam said. "But which song?"

They talked for an hour about various songs, but in the end, at Michelle's suggestion, they chose a Disney song that had four characters in it. Karen had some fantastic costume suggestions. They finally had a talent show plan.

Miriam's aunt and uncle had a few ideas about how the Kindness Club could connect with the orphanage. They would connect more kids and orphans for pen pals. They could also raise money for supplies and presents or collect donated items for the orphans for Christmas. They said that even cards would be a great idea since it would cost a lot to mail a package to Kenya. If they wanted to collect items for donation, it would be cheaper to do that closer to the summer so they could check them as luggage when they returned. Miriam took the email with her to the next Kindness Club meeting.

"We were just saying at the staff meeting last week that the school needed a big service project. I think this idea would be fantastic," Mr. Mitchell said after Miriam told the Kindness Club about the email from her aunt and uncle. He was their club sponsor and taught art class. "I think this could be something the school could be involved with long-term. We could do cards and fundraising at Christmas and collect supplies whenever your aunt and uncle come to visit. We could set up a pen pal program, too."

"What if we did Hat Fridays to raise money?" one boy in the group suggested.

"I think that's a great idea," Sydney agreed. "I was thinking maybe we could sell holiday grams before Christmas, then people could spread kindness here, and the money could help the orphanage over there."

Miriam smiled as the whole club brainstormed ways they could raise money to help an orphanage in Kenya. She'd have to email her aunt and uncle and Gasira tonight and tell them the good news. They had to get final approval from the principal, but Mr. Mitchell made it sound like he knew she would love the idea.

They ended up doing three fundraisers in November and December. They did the Hat Fridays, when students could wear a hat to school if they paid $1 for each Friday in both months. They also did Thanksgiving and Christmas candy grams. Students could choose an encouraging message and a piece of candy to send to another student for $1. They raised $2,085 in those two months. Some people donated more than $1 because they knew it was supporting the orphanage. Mr. Mitchell surprised them at their first Kindness Club meeting in December with an extra $575 donated by the teachers and staff. Miriam's aunt had been in touch with Mr. Mitchell and the principal and had set up how to transfer the money online so the orphanage could receive the money two weeks before Christmas. Aunt Susan had written and told Miriam that if they got an extra $1,000, they could buy a small present for each child. Miriam wished she could see her aunt's reaction when she got almost three times that amount.

The students had also made cards that were being mailed next week. The Kindness Club had gathered a list of students interested in having a pen pal and would be sending that to Miriam's aunt and uncle as well. The orphans would make contact in January to start up the pen pal relationship.

The Kindness Club had everything wrapped up the week before school got out so they could focus on their finals. Miriam had reduced her piano practice time to only 30 minutes a day for the past few weeks so she could study, work on her paper for English, create a presentation for science, practice for her choir singing test, and help with the Kindness Club project. She was looking forward to winter break and just enjoying some time relaxing and spending time with her grandma.

All of Miriam's friends except Karen went out of town for Christmas. Even Steph's parents had taken some time off work, although they decided to go to Vail even though Steph couldn't ski yet. Her cast had been removed, but physical therapy was moving slowly, and she was supposed to be careful with her activity level until mid-February. Sydney, Anna, and Michelle all went to visit their grandparents in various states. Grace's family was taking a vacation to Hawaii as a Christmas present to them all. Karen and Miriam got together a few times to hang out or go shopping at the mall.

Grandma invited a few more people to Christmas dinner than the previous year. They set up an extra folding table in the living room to accommodate everyone. There had been several deaths of older people in the church during the past year, and Grandma invited anyone who was newly widowed for Christmas dinner. Miriam had fun baking and prepping all the food with Grandma. They put on Christmas music while they worked and made sure to take Christmas movie breaks — Grandma had an entire shelf dedicated to just Christmas movies.

Miriam recognized almost everyone who came to dinner, and helped her grandma host. They had spent a quiet morning opening a few presents. Miriam had gotten her grandma a new hat, gloves and scarf set in a pretty teal color — her favorite. She also bought her a few books. Miriam was surprised that her present was a phone. She had assumed that Grandma would get her one when she was older or that she'd have to buy one herself.

"I think it's time you learned how to use one of these responsibly," Grandma said. "We'll talk about rules tomorrow, but you can spend today getting it all set up and ready to use."

Miriam thanked her and opened a card from her aunt and uncle, which contained a gift card to a local bookshop. Miriam was happy with her presents. Having contact with Gasira put Christmas into perspective for her. She was glad she could live with relatives and not worry about food, clothing, or getting presents for holidays and birthdays. Living in an orphanage would be hard and lonely.

Miriam practiced piano for one to two hours a day during the Christmas break. She almost had the song she wanted to play for the talent show memorized and had a good grasp on the one her friends wanted to sing. She was glad Mrs. Ritzer said she could do both for the talent show. Her friends had a plan to practice every Friday night. Michelle and Karen were working on costumes for them to wear and were even planning something special for Miriam to wear for her performance. Steph finally had no crutches or brace by the end of February, and while she was still in physical therapy for another month or so, the doctor said she could do normal activities, except for cheer and running. Miriam usually performed her piece each Friday night to practice being in front of a crowd. Grandma planned to videotape the performance so her aunt and uncle could watch it. They were really looking forward to "seeing" her perform. When she lived with them, her aunt often told her how much she loved hearing Miriam play the piano.

The school decided to have the talent show after school on the Thursday before spring break. There would be a donation bucket for the orphanage and a collection center for supply donations. They really needed outdoor sports gear, books, and school supplies. A few times a week, Miriam would have a student stop her in the hall and tell her how much they liked having a pen pal and ask if there was anything they could be doing to help the orphanage. Miriam was glad to have started something so worthwhile at her school.

The girls all met at Sydney's house after school that Thursday for one last practice. Michelle and Karen gave them all vests that had red sequins all over the front except for silver ones on the left in the shape of the first letter of their name. They had also made matching fingerless gloves for Miriam to wear when she did her piece. They ran through both pieces twice and then headed home for a quick dinner. They met back up at school in the music room.

Mrs. Ritzer was pacing the floor and staring at her phone. She stopped when it buzzed, letting her know she was getting a call. She hurriedly walked to her desk in the corner to take the call. It was brief, but Miriam noticed she looked worried when she got off the phone. She shook her head, stood up, and got the students' attention.

"If you had planned to have piano accompaniment with your act, please come see me," she announced. Miriam walked over since she was the accompanist for her friends, but she wasn't sure if that was what Mrs. Ritzer meant.

"I have some bad news," Mrs. Ritzer told the three students who came to her desk with Miriam. "Our accompanist is sick and can't come tonight. I could try and play your songs, but I'm honestly not a very good piano player. I usually need to practice a song a lot before I can play it. Would you be willing to sing a capella?"

"You mean sing without the music?" one girl asked. "I don't think I can."

"What songs are you guys singing?" Miriam asked. "I might be able to help."

The students showed Miriam their pieces, and fortunately, they were all pretty basic songs.

"Mrs. Ritzer, if you can make me copies of their music and give me a few minutes to play through them, I can play the music for them."

"Oh, Miriam, that would be wonderful!" Mrs. Ritzer replied. "I'll go make copies right away, then I'll open the band room for you to practice."

Miriam went back and told her friends what she would be doing and then she went with Mrs. Ritzer to the band room. They had 20 minutes until the show was due to start. Mrs. Ritzer would come to get her when there was five minutes left. Miriam went through each song twice and felt confident that she could play them well enough for the other students to sing while she played.

"Welcome to the Bristolway Middle School Talent Show!" Mrs. Ritzer announced at the show's start. "Tonight, we have a special addition that is not on your program. Our pianist is not feeling well so one of our talented students will play the accompaniment for Taylor, Spencer and Kelsey instead — Miriam Stanley. Thank you, Miriam!"

The crowd applauded, and the first act started. Taylor and Spencer were the fourth and fifth acts. Her friends would sing a few acts after that, and then it was Kelsey's song. Miriam's performance was the very last one, and she received a long round of applause. She had a few mistakes in some of the music but just moved on in the piece to keep the flow going. She hoped most people wouldn't be able to pick them out.

There was a small break after the acts for the judges to confer before they announced the winners. The performing students had to wait behind the stage curtain. Her friends couldn't stop telling Miriam how good she was, playing all those songs. After what felt like a long time to Miriam, the curtain went up.

"We want to thank everyone who participated in the talent show," Mrs. Ritzer said. "We have some very talented students at this school. I want to point out that we raised $368 and had several supply donations for the orphanage in Kenya our school has partnered with. Thank you to everyone who helped support that effort.

"Our third-place winner tonight is Miriam Stanley!"

Miriam was stunned. She honestly thought several other acts were better than hers, but she walked forward and received a small trophy from Mrs. Ritzer.

"Our second-place winner is Kyle Griffith. After a lot of hard deliberation, our first-place winner is Taylor Duncan."

The crowd applauded, then Taylor walked over to Miriam.

"I wouldn't have won if you hadn't offered to play the piano for my song. I can't sing well without music. Let's switch trophies — you deserve first place."

Miriam didn't know what to say. This was beyond she had wished for. She hadn't even wished to win anything but just wanted to play well, and now she was being offered the first-place spot.

"Thank you, Taylor, but I'm fine with my third-place trophy. I was glad to help you out. You have a wonderful voice," Miriam said. Taylor hugged her, and they walked off the stage together.

"I'm so proud of you, Miriam!" Grandma cried as she hugged her when she got off the stage. "You truly have a great heart to offer to play those songs tonight. Great talent, too."

"Thank you! All that practice finally paid off for something really good," Miriam replied.

"Yes, it did — something very good."

Miriam put her trophy next to the picture of her parents on her nightstand. She knew they would have been proud of what she had done tonight. She was smiling as she drifted off to sleep.

After spring break, the Kindness Club went to work collecting donations for the orphanage. The cost of boxing up the items and paying an extra baggage fee was cheaper than mailing them. Many people gave money, and the club did a few more Hat Fridays and a Spring Gram that was like the Thanksgiving and Christmas grams.

At the end of April, it was time for freshman orientation. The high school was only a few blocks from the middle school, but it was raining, so the eighth graders were bussed over one Friday. They had an itinerary for the day that included an assembly, tours, lunch at the high school, and sitting in a few classes and one elective. The students were divided up into groups based on the elective they picked. Miriam was with Steph, Sydney, and Anna as they had all chosen choir. Michelle and Grace were going to check out art, while Karen wanted to try out for the high school band. Her parents had let her take flute lessons to see how she liked it, and she was really enjoying it.

"Welcome to Bristolway High School, home of the winning Bearcats! I'm the principal here at the high school, and you can call me Mr. Sherman. To my right is the Vice Principal, Mrs. Rennar and to my left is our counselor, Ms. Tuttle.

"We have heard good things about you and are excited to have you join us as freshmen in a few months. Today you will get a taste of how things work at the high school. Next week, you will fill out your class choices so that we can get schedules to you before the school year ends. You will start school one day earlier than the rest of the high school to give you a day to find all your classes without all the crowds.

"In a minute, we'll break you up into groups and start your day. You will get to sit in two classes, one special, and have a tour of the entire school grounds. Before your lunch period, you will come back here and get a chance to see what clubs, sports, and extracurricular activities we offer.

"The tour guides will be down here with signs, so when I dismiss you, go to your assigned tour guide. But, before we do that, let's do the Bearcat cheer!"

The eighth-graders all stood up and did the cheer. There was a sense of excitement and nervousness among the students. Moving up to high school seemed like a huge milestone to Miriam. Four more years and then she would be going to college and doing adult things.

"Okay, choir girls, let's go join Group B," Sydney said as the cheer died down. "Have fun, Michelle, Grace, and Karen — we'll see you at the end of the day."

Miriam was glad to have three friends with her in her group.

"I'm almost glad I broke my leg," Steph said to Miriam. "Look at how those cheer girls aren't talking to anyone but themselves. I think I'm going to stick with choir. Do you think they have a Kindness Club here at the high school?"

"I don't know, but we can find out before lunch. We could always start one if there isn't one. I think that club was one of my favorite parts of middle school."

The tour guide began to speak to the group, so Miriam and Steph stopped talking and paid attention.

"Hi, incoming freshman. I'm Sammie, and I'm a senior here. I was told you are in this group because you want to see our choir. Well, I want to tell you that we actually have three choirs! We have a general classic choir that all grades can join, but it's the only one open to freshmen. Then, we have two choirs you can audition for when you are in 10th grade or higher — show choir and an a cappella group. I'm in show choir. Choir is at the end of the day, so we'll see that last.

First thing up is a math class and then a science class. We have the first lunch period, so we'll see the clubs and then eat after science. After lunch is the school tour, then choir before you head back to the middle school. Any questions?"

No one had any questions, so Sammie started leading the way out of the gym. She was wearing a Bristolway letter jacket that was brown with orange shoulder cuffs and wristbands. There was orange along the bottom of the jacket and an orange music note under her orange embroidered name. She was wearing jeans, a T-shirt, and sneakers.

"Do you think I could do my hair like hers?" Sydney asked Miriam. Sammie's hair had several small braids tied into a side French braid.

"Yes — let's practice tonight at your house. It looks cute," Miriam replied.

"Please be quiet as we're walking through the halls," Sammie told the group, as many of them had been whispering back and forth.

They had to stand along the walls or sit on the floor in the science and math classes. Science was just the general freshman science, but math was pre-calculus. Miriam was lost listening to what the teacher was talking about. She was in pre-algebra this year and would take algebra as a freshman. Karen was in the class with her, and they hoped they would get the same class next year, too. There seemed to be a lot to learn before she got to pre-calculus.

The girls could talk to each other again when they got back to the gym. They walked by all the club exhibits together and saw several fun possibilities. There was sewing club, chess club, writing club, art club, and computer coding club. They didn't see anything that resembled the Kindness Club and started talking at lunch about starting one up at the high school.

"We could talk to Anna tonight and have her ask her brother which teacher would be a good sponsor," Michelle said.

"Great idea!" Sydney replied. "I already see some kids who eat alone, so I bet the club would go over well here. I loved it when we had our 'No One Eats Alone Day.' I think it really opened up people's eyes to how many people sat by themselves at lunch."

"More kindness never hurts," Miriam said. "I say we do it, but we can see if everyone agrees tonight."

Lunch went by quickly, but that may have been because the girls had so many more options to decide from for lunch. There was always pizza, bagels, a salad bar, sandwiches, and a hot lunch option. Middle school only had a hot lunch or pre-made salad.

After lunch, they got a tour of the entire school. The building was two stories high and looked like an X. One hallway had math on the first floor and science on the second floor. Another had English classes on the first floor and social studies and some special classes on the second floor. Along with the rest of the special classes, the cafeteria was down another hallway, with the special classes being on top. The last hallway was where the gym and music classes were; this was open to the top of the second floor. The rain had stopped, so Sammie also took them outside to point out all the sports fields and the marching band field. There was also a field for classes to use for experiments or projects, or when teachers felt like holding a class outside.

After the tour, they went to choir and were able to join in the warm-ups. The a cappella and show choirs came in to perform a song each, then the general choir sang a few songs for them. The teacher, Mr. Nuskett, seemed very confident and encouraging. Miriam felt the most comfortable in that classroom of any place she had been in the high school that day.

Sammie took them directly to the busses when choir ended, and they headed back to the middle school. They had just a minute to chat at their lockers before heading home, but since it was Friday, they would all meet up at Sydney's that night.

They had all agreed to figure out a way to start a Kindness Club at the high school. Anna checked with her brother, and he actually recommended Mr. Nuskett. They planned to talk to him on the first day of school if they got a chance.

The middle school held an assembly to give out awards the week before school ended. They did seventh and eighth grades separately. Karen got on the honor roll, and Miriam, Sydney, and Anna were recognized for good grades.

The assembly was just about over when Mrs. Traine surprised Miriam by calling the Kindness Club up on the stage.

"It's not often that you have students who decide to put others first in the ways the Kindness Club did this year. Our school is now forever tied to the orphans in Kenya, and we are committed to helping them for as many years as we can. I think all of us have become better at thinking about how we could help those in need. Many of you now have a pen pal in Kenya and have been changed by that friendship. Please keep in contact with that person as you move on to high school and through life.

Miriam Stanley, thank you for bringing us the idea. We would like to give this certificate to you and all the Kindness Club members for bringing a very worthwhile cause to our school."

Everyone in the audience stood up and applauded the club, while Miriam and her friends smiled and accepted their certificates. Mrs. Traine dismissed them to go back to class. As Miriam and her friends walked back, many people came up to them and personally thanked them for organizing the aid for the orphanage. Miriam hadn't quite realized until then how many people had been impacted by the idea of helping the orphanage. It had definitely been worthwhile. She would be telling her aunt and uncle all about it in her email this weekend. They would be here in less than two months, and she was really looking forward to seeing them.

Chapter 9

Miriam's summer looked a lot like the previous year's summer, except Steph came over even more often. It was nice for both of the girls to have someone else around. Grandma still kept up all her activities in the summer, and some of them even required more time, such as the Master Gardeners. Miriam did the book club again, but instead of picking certain books, the group would just get together and discuss what books they had been reading. Miriam only invited the kids who had shown up last summer.

Her aunt and uncle arrived on July 1. They would spend the Fourth of July with Miriam and her grandmother, then head up to Nebraska on July 13 to visit family there. They would fly back to Kenya out of Kansas City so they could stay one final night with them before flying back and take the school donations with them when they left. They arrived at almost 9 p.m., so they were very tired on the ride home. They all chatted a little about how the flights were, what movies and books they'd watched, and how much sleep they'd managed to get. However, Miriam could see that any talk about her life or the orphanage would have to wait until Uncle Mike and Aunt Susan had a good night's sleep.

They slept in until 10 a.m. the next day. Miriam had woken up at 7 a.m. and read some after breakfast, waiting for her aunt and uncle to wake up. Grandma had cleared almost everything off her calendar for the next two weeks, but she said she would still try to get some swimming in for exercise — not today, though.

Miriam gave her aunt and uncle big hugs when they came downstairs from the guest room, which was across from her room. Those two rooms and a bathroom were the entire upstairs apart from the attic. Grandma's room was downstairs down a hallway behind the stairs.

"What would you like for breakfast?" Grandma asked.

"You don't happen to have any cold pizza?" Uncle Mike asked, smiling. He was wearing a Kenyan soccer shirt and black sweatpants. "I think I might be jet-lagged."

"How about eggs and toast?" she proposed. "And coffee?"

"That would be wonderful," Aunt Susan said.

"So, Miriam, it sounds like you've been having a good time living here with your grandma. What shall we do while we're here?"

"I thought I'd introduce you to my friends at some point, then I have some songs I wanted to play for you on the piano. We could go to the swim park, too, or ..." Miriam looked at Grandma, "... Steph said yesterday that Rogers and Hammerstein's Cinderella is playing at the theater downtown."

"I'm not sure how much those tickets cost," she replied. "But we can look into it. Here's breakfast!"

The time with Aunt Susan and Uncle Mike passed by quicker than Miriam wanted. Besides that first day, they had company over every night — mostly friends of her aunt and uncle from work and church. They asked Miriam to play the piano for all of their guests after dinner. Miriam could tell they were showing her off in a way. Miriam had some of the stories from the orphanage memorized by the time the two weeks were up. One night, though, her friends came over for dinner. Unfortunately, Karen was away in California for her summer vacation, and Michelle didn't feel well that night. She could tell her aunt and uncle really liked her friends, which made Miriam very happy. They had played the part of her "parents" for a while, and their opinion would always matter a lot to Miriam.

After dinner on their last night before heading to Omaha, Aunt Susan pulled Miriam aside.

"Your grandma told me that she gave you a box of your parents' things," she said. "Have you looked through it much? I wanted to see if you had any questions about the meaning behind some of those things."

"It's up in my closet," Miriam told her. "I tried looking through it a few times, but I got really sad, so I stopped. There are some photo albums, journals, an empty jewelry box, and a few books."

"I helped Grandma chose those things. They were mostly what your parents had on their nightstands, which is where people usually keep the items they use often. Did she tell you she has your parents' jewelry?"

"No, she didn't," Miriam replied.

"Oh, well, don't ask about it. I think she might give it to you on another birthday. Can I show you something about that jewelry box, though?"

"Sure," Miriam agreed. "Want to go up to my room?"

"Yes, let's do that."

They walked to Miriam's room without speaking, and Miriam went right to the closet to get the jewelry box. It was a dark, polished wooden box that opened to a space divided into four sections with green felt at the bottom of each section. There was nothing marked on the outside or inside. She handed it to her aunt. Aunt Susan closed the box, squeezed the two sides with one hand, and then opened it with the other. She then reached in and grabbed the middle of the divider, and it came out!

"This jewelry box was made by your grandpa at your mother's request for you when you were a baby," Aunt Susan said. "She wanted a false bottom so you would have a hiding spot, especially if you ended up with a sibling."

Aunt Susan showed Miriam what was in the hidden compartment — papers.

"I checked it before we packed it away and saw there were notes in the jewelry box. I imagine your mother wanted you to find them when she gave you the jewelry box as a gift. I'm not sure when she planned to do it, but I thought you're old enough now at 14.

"You don't have to read them now, but I wanted to show you they were there in person."

Miriam had been staring at the notes the entire time her aunt was talking. She finally looked up at her with some tears in her eyes.

Her aunt reached over, wiped a tear from Miriam's cheek, and tucked a string of brown curls behind Miriam's ear.

"They loved you so much, Miribug," Aunt Susan told her. "We do, too. I'll give you a few minutes."

She kissed the top of Miriam's head and left Miriam alone in her room. Miriam decided to at least read one of the notes right then.

Dear Miribug,

I can't believe eight years have already gone by! I've enjoyed each and every day that you've been with us. It seems like you were just a tiny baby yesterday, and yet, sometimes, when I look at you, I get glimpses of the woman you will become. You have such a caring heart, and I am often amazed at how you see this world. The good seems to always jump up at you first. You teach Mommy and Daddy so much every day.

Keep growing and learning and being kind!

Love you,

Mom

Miriam held the letter to her heart and started crying harder. She could hear her mom's voice as she read the letter. She quickly looked at the rest of the letters; the next one was in her dad's handwriting. Her parents must have written her a letter on each of her birthdays. She quickly realized what a treasure she had with those letters. She found a tissue and dried her eyes. She would read the letter from her dad tonight and save the rest for another day. It would be tough enough saying goodbye to her aunt and uncle tomorrow. She knew she would see them for a few hours before they flew back to Kenya in two weeks, but having them here reminded her of all the love they had shown her after her parents had died. The people she loved always seemed to be leaving.

Right after Uncle Mike and Aunt Susan left the next morning, Grandma asked Miriam to join her in her bedroom.

"Susan told me she showed you the jewelry box last night," she said. "I had thought I would give you your parents' jewelry when you were 16, but you are very mature and responsible at 14, and I see no reason to make you wait. Especially since you now know how special your jewelry box is."

She opened her closet and grabbed a small box off the top shelf. She handed it to Miriam, who sat on Grandma's bed before opening it. She saw her parents' wedding rings, high school class rings, a pair of diamond earrings and matching necklace, and a pair of emerald earrings with a matching necklace. There was also an emerald ring. Her parents' watches were also in the box.

"I knew they would want to you have these. Besides the high school rings, the jewelry is all gifts they gave each other," Grandma said.

Miriam picked up her dad's watch and looked at the back of the face. It was engraved with his initials and their wedding date. She looked at each of their plain gold wedding bands and saw "Always" engraved on the inside of each.

"I'm so glad you kept these, Grandma," Miriam told her. "I will treasure them."

"I know you will. If you ever want company when you go through the box of your parents' things or have any questions, let me know. I love you, Miriam."

"I love you, too, Grandma."

Miriam went up to her room and put the jewelry in her jewelry box that now sat on her nightstand next to her parents' picture. She had moved her trophy to the top of her dresser. Year by year, it seemed like her parents were closer to her rather than moving farther away in her memory.

The day before Uncle Mike and Aunt Susan came back, Miriam's friends came over and helped her box up all the donations for the orphanage. Anna was the only one out of town that day. Their goal was to keep it to four boxes, and after three attempts, they finally got everything to fit — barely. They rewarded themselves with ice cream sundaes.

"Less than a month until we're freshmen," Steph said as they started eating their sundaes.

"I'm kind of nervous," Karen replied.

"Me, too," Michelle announced. "We really lucked out because we know someone in almost all of our classes."

"Very true!" Sydney said. "I only don't have any of you in my gym class."

"I'm only on my own in band," Karen commented.

"I think computer class is the only one I have on my own, but I've been working on coding this summer with an online program," Steph told them.

"We all have the same lunch, too," Miriam said. "I think we'll do just fine."

They had an end-of-summer sleepover at Sydney's house the Friday before school began. Freshmen would start on Tuesday, and the rest of the high school would join them on Wednesday. Miriam was really glad they had a whole day to themselves to figure out how to get from class to class; it felt like the tour happened a long time ago!

Miriam, Steph, Sydney, and Anna told Mr. Nuskett their idea about starting a Kindness Club right before choir class started. He asked them to come during their lunch period on Friday to talk about more details. However, it definitely sounded like something he would like to help sponsor.

Miriam felt so tired by the end of the first day of school, and it wasn't from figuring out how to get from class to class. Once she started remembering the layout, it was pretty easy to find the hallway she was supposed to be in. She was overwhelmed by the syllabi that the teachers had passed out. The only classes that would be "easy" were choir and gym. She had homework in every class the first night, too. Granted, most were fairly simple or worksheets about the subjects, but almost every teacher said there would be nightly homework, weekly quizzes or tests, and quarterly projects. Between school, piano, and starting up Kindness Club, Miriam wasn't sure she'd have much time for anything else. She wanted to join the coding club with Steph, but she decided to see how school went the first quarter before joining.

Miriam had more B's in her classes at the beginning of October than she would like, but she decided to study really hard to try and bring them up before the end of the quarter. Her friends were also struggling under the heavier homework loads, so they had decided to get together every other Friday this year instead of every Friday. Someone was usually busy each of the times, but they tried hard to keep up their Friday gatherings going for now. They did sit together at lunch every day when they didn't have any clubs or projects, extra choir practice, or a study session. At least they all were able to make it to Miriam's 15th birthday party on Friday. Her birthday wouldn't be until Wednesday, but she was very conscious about making sure she didn't have any plans the night she would go to the island. She usually had piano lessons on Wednesdays, but Grandma had relented and canceled that one lesson so Miriam could get all her homework done before the door to the island opened.

Only Sydney and Steph could spend the night after her birthday party. The rest had early morning plans on Saturday and were getting picked up by 9 a.m. It would be a fun party, though. Grandma had let Miriam organize a painting party and had bought everyone canvas, a paint set with brushes, and a painting apron. She had found instructions on how to paint a fox, and Grandma offered to be their instructor. She even got a fox cake from the grocery store bakery. Miriam decided that a fox might be her new favorite animal.

Grandma told her she would wait and give her a present on her actual birthday. Her friends had all pitched in and got her a charm bracelet with a music note, book, fox, and "M" charms on it. Miriam put it on right away and hugged each of her friends. They painted and ate cake and ice cream. After Anna, Michelle, and Karen left, Miriam, Steph, and Sydney watched a movie before settling in to "sleep." They actually talked about school and boys until two in the morning, but they were quiet, and Grandma never came out to remind them to lower their voices or go to sleep. They woke up around 8 a.m., though, to the smell of pancakes and bacon. Miriam smiled — Grandma saved bacon for special occasions.

Miriam had Grandma look up her grades before she headed to school on her birthday. She had brought her math grade up to an A, but science and social studies were still B's. There was only one week to go in the quarter, and Miriam decided right then that she would wish for good grades tonight on the island. She was already working hard, but it still wasn't quite enough. She had only gotten one B before in sixth grade, and that was because of an assignment she had done but had forgotten to turn in. Her teacher had given her partial credit when she turned it in late. She wanted straight A's still, and maybe the wish would help fix the gap between her work and getting the grades she wanted.

When she got home from school, there were three presents for her on the table. Grandma had stayed home from swim class to celebrate Miriam's birthday. She made Miriam's favorite — spaghetti and meatballs with garlic bread — and they had some ice cream that was left over from her party. Only after they were done eating would she let Miriam open her presents.

The largest one was first, and it was a beautiful fox stuffed animal. The second was a journal with a big purple M on the cover, and the last present was a 24-pack of gel pens.

"I think you're old enough to start recording your thoughts," Grandma told her. "Who knows — you might be famous one day, and people will pay good money to find out what you thought about when you were 15? Or, maybe your children will want to know you better. When you feel up to it, I think you'll find you know your mom even better after you read her journals. When the time is right, you'll know it."

"Thank you, Grandma. I'll start writing tonight," Miriam told her. "It's hard spending so much time thinking about my parents. Is that wrong?"

"No, Miriam. It means you loved them very much and still do. I think it may be harder since you hear their voices every year on the island. Often, memories and grief fade with time, but you bring them back to life in a way every year when you go to the island."

"It's the same with the photos, letters, and journals," Miriam continued. "When I try to look at them, it feels like they're right in the next room, not gone forever."

"No one is really gone forever," Grandma said. "Every person we love lives in our hearts. I don't tell you, but I think of Grandpa every day. I have pictures of us everywhere in this house, and sometimes I think he's just at work and will come home at the end of the day."

"Oh, Grandma, I'm so glad you understand!" Miriam hugged her and wiped the few tears that had fallen on her cheeks. They hugged each other for a little longer than usual but were both smiling by the time they pulled away.

"It is nice to have a soul that understands, even though we both wish it were different," Grandma said. "I have one last present for you — I'll do the dishes. Why don't you get ready for the island? If I'm asleep again when you get back, I hope you sleep well tonight. Can't wait to hear how your visit goes."

"Love you, Grandma."

"Love you, too, my Miriam."

Miriam took her fox, journal, and pens with her up to her room. It was almost time to visit the island.

Miriam tried to read as she waited for the street lamps to flicker. She couldn't make herself focus on the words, though. She was anxious to get to the island. When the glowing words appeared on the attic door, she was reminded of her mom's emerald ring. She opened her jewelry box and put it on before opening the attic door.

She couldn't help but smile as she stepped onto the sand of the island again. She closed the door behind her, and a slight breeze blew a few curls across her face. She only saw one person standing by the big tree, and she started walking towards her. As she got closer, Miriam saw it was Lexi.

Before she reached Lexi, she heard footsteps behind her and saw Amelia running across the sand. She wondered if Aaron would show up. He was usually there before her most years.

"Hi, Lexi. Hi, Amelia," Miriam said. "Have a good year?"

"It was pretty good," Lexi replied. "I found some new friends, finally."

"I got first place in my gymnastics competition," Amelia announced.

"Congrats!" Miriam remarked.

"How about you?" Lexi asked.

"I got third place in our school talent show but was able to be a last-minute accompanist when the main one called in sick," Miriam replied.

"Wow, you must be pretty good at the piano then," Amelia said.

"Hello, my dears," a familiar voice said from above them. Stella fluttered down to the ground and looked them all over.

"Only three? We started with six. There used to be more magic in the world. More smiles. More wonder. I remember when we would have 300 children show up each year," Stella said. "Well, I will wait again and hope the young man shows up this year. You may go ahead with your wishing."

Miriam looked hard at Stella before she went to get her Starfruit. She didn't seem as bright and glowing as she usually did. Maybe it was because Miriam was getting older and finding it harder to believe in magic. She would have to ask Stella before she left.

Miriam found her Starfruit easily, walked to a spot where there was sand and sunshine, and sat down. She took a bite and wished for good grades this year. Then, she heard her parents' voices.

"We love you more than the world! Be good and be kind," her mom said.

"And be smart, Miribug," her dad said. "Bye."

Miriam sat there with her eyes closed for longer than any other time she had been on the island. She had been fiddling with her mom's emerald ring while she listened to their message. She had felt her parents with her more this past year than at any other time since they had died. When Miriam opened her eyes, she decided this would be the year she would go through her parents' things and read their notes. She had now lived without them for seven years and needed to learn more about who they were.

As she stood up to go bury her Starfruit, Stella came over and helped Miriam dig the hole.

"Don't take this the wrong way," Miriam told Stella, "but are you fading? You don't see to glow as much as you did last year."

"I'm surprised you could notice," Stella said. "We can only survive if people believe in magic. With fewer orphans opening the door to the island, the harder it is for us to shine. It's like our power is draining. There are a few Volturians who can't leave our main city anymore because they've faded so much they can't fly."

"Oh, Stella, that is so sad. Is there anything I can do to help you?"

"You are a sweet, special child, Miriam," Stella replied. "The best thing you can do is to keep believing in magic and keep coming back every year. We get a special boost of power when children come back for their final visit to hear their parents' wishes."

"I will come back, Stella. Although, I have to admit my main motivation is to hear my parents' voices. Even if there were no wishes, I would come for that."

Stella smiled, and Miriam noticed Stella started glowing a little bit brighter after she said that.

"Ready to head home?" Stella asked as they finished burying the Starfruit.

"Yes," Miriam said. "I'll be back next year."

Miriam stepped back into her room and looked around. The house was quiet. With the TV off, she knew her grandma had already gone to bed. She almost didn't check the attic door but had to make sure the island wasn't still accessible. She would go back in a heartbeat. However, when she opened up the attic door, it was just the attic. She put the ring back in her jewelry box, got ready for bed, and then lay in bed, staring at her parents' photo for a long time, finally falling asleep to dream about the island.

Chapter 10

Miriam got her report card the next week and was ecstatic to get all A's. She was relieved and felt like she finally had a feel for how high school should work. Her friends managed to get some pretty good grades, too, so they decided to try going back to meeting every Friday night. Miriam still worked hard on her homework each night but found herself spending more time playing the piano after school and less time worrying about how her grades would turn out. She and Gasira were writing to each other a few times a week. Gasira had gotten into the local public school, and they both had heavy homework loads. Gasira even joined the choir at her school, so they had a lot in common to talk about. She was writing to her aunt and uncle every weekend, too.

Report cards for the second quarter were passed out in their last classes on the last day of school before winter break. Miriam opened hers and couldn't believe her grades.

"This can't be right," Miriam whispered to herself. She quickly put the report card back in the envelope and stuck it in her book bag. She looked over at Steph, who gave her a thumbs-up. Steph's parents had said she could only get one B, or she would be grounded from television and friends for two weeks. Miriam wondered what Grandma would say and do to her when she saw the report card.

On the bus ride home, Miriam deflected Steph's questions about her report card. Miriam told her she had a headache and didn't feel like talking much. Steph patted her shoulder and let Miriam be.

Miriam tried to play the piano when she got home. Grandma wouldn't be home from swim class for another hour. Miriam couldn't concentrate, so she pulled the report card out of her backpack to look at it again. Maybe she had seen the grades wrong. She laid it on the table and saw that she hadn't seen it wrong at all. She had a few A's, but those were in choir and gym. She had B's in social studies, science, and English, and she had a C in math. She had never seen a C on her report card! The more she stared at the grades, the angrier she got. Didn't she wish for good grades? What had happened? She had done all her homework and turned it in on time. Were the Volturians just offering wishes to increase their power but not really granting them?

Her anger turned to tears, and she sat down at the table. Would her grandma ground her?

Just then, Grandma walked in.

"Hello, Miriam. I'm home," Grandma said and then she walked into the kitchen and saw Miriam crying at the table. She came over and sat down next to her.

"What's wrong, Miri?"

Miriam pushed the report card toward her then put her head down in her arms. She didn't want to see her grandma's disappointed face.

"Miriam, look at me," Grandma said. Miriam looked up.

"I know these grades are not what you expected, but B's are not so bad. For many people, they are very good grades. Do you know how you got a C in math, though? You've always been great at math."

"I'm not sure, Grandma," Miriam said. "I did all my homework, turned it in on time, and studied for all the tests."

"Did you work as hard as you did in the first quarter?"

"Well, I felt like I was doing well, so I spent more time each day practicing piano and wrote longer messages to Gasira and Aunt Susan and Uncle Mike. I may have relaxed a little bit, but I don't feel like I slacked off."

"Well, you might have to get back into the habit of studying harder again. Let's see how you do next quarter, but there are three things we are going to do now. Your grades are a little more important now that you're in high school. Colleges will see these grades when you start applying. Let's limit piano to no more than 30 minutes a day, limit emailing people in Kenya to only two times a week, and we're going to get you a math tutor."

"I'm not grounded?"

"No, but if you don't pull your math grade up, then I might have to limit your time with friends. You have to have some down time, though. I know how important your friends are to you."

Miriam hugged her grandma. Her plan sounded good, and Miriam knew she could bring her grades back up quickly.

Grandma said the new rules wouldn't begin until school started, so Miriam spent the Christmas break playing a lot of piano, hanging out with Steph when she was in town, writing long emails to Gasira, her aunt and uncle, and reading. The crowd for Christmas dinner was a bit smaller this year than last, as a few of the widows had remarried, and others had moved closer to their children. Miriam still enjoyed being able to do something nice for others at Christmas. Her grandma had got her several books and a new study planner for her for Christmas. Miriam got her grandma a new swim bag with her initials embroidered on it. Her Aunt Susan and Uncle Mike had sent a photo book with photos from the orphanage that showed the kids opening their Christmas gifts from last year and playing with them. It also showed them opening and using the sports equipment they had taken back with them on the plane. The last few pages were photos of Gasira that showed a day in her life. Grandma had suggested she stop by the middle school one day to show the principal.

Sydney had everyone over for a sleepover the last Friday before school started back up. They did a $10 gift swap and discussed Christmas presents and New Year's resolutions. Miriam finally told her friends about her grades and how she would have to get a tutor.

"I had a tutor last year," Michelle said. "It was for science, but Adrian was really nice and helped me out a lot. They have a program at the high school where some juniors and seniors volunteer to help tutor other kids. I think they get volunteer hours for the National Honor Society for doing it. They can come to your house, or you can meet with them after school."

"That would be great," Miriam replied. "I think it would be better to use a free program. Grandma shouldn't have to pay for me to get help since it's my fault I let my grades slide."

"Mrs. Whitfield is the contact at the high school. She teaches 12th grade literature class," Michelle told her.

"Thanks, Michelle," Miriam said. "I'll tell Grandma, then talk to Mrs. Whitfield when school starts."

Miriam was so glad none of her friends gave her a hard time because of her bad grades. She definitely had found the right group to count as friends! She felt better knowing Michelle had been tutored as well. Michelle was pretty smart, and even she needed help!

The girls spent the rest of the night talking and watching movies.

Grandma had really liked the idea of a free tutor from school. Miriam talked to Mrs. Whitfield before school on the first day back and was told they tried to do sessions after school on Thursdays. If Miriam checked in on Thursday after school, Mrs. Whitfield would have a student there to help tutor Miriam in math. Grandma had already said she could pick Miriam up from school any day that would work. Thursday would be great, as Miriam wouldn't have to change her Wednesday piano lesson.

When Miriam showed up at Mrs. Whitfield's class on Thursday after school, there were about 12 students already sitting in the class. Miriam went up to Mrs. Whitfield to find out who her tutor would be.

"Amy, can you come up here, please?" Mrs. Whitfield called to a group of older students in the back of the class.

"Miriam, this is Amy. She'll be able to tutor you in math. You're in algebra, right?" Mrs. Whitefield asked Miriam.

"Yes, I'm in algebra," Miriam said.

"Great," Amy said. "I love math. Do you want to stay in here or go sit out in the cafeteria area?"

"It seems pretty crowded in here. Do you mind if we go to the cafeteria?" Miriam asked.

"Don't mind at all," Amy said. "Follow me."

Miriam followed Amy to the cafeteria. Amy was wearing a French braid in her long brown hair. She wore jeans, cowboy boots, and a pink and purple plaid button-up shirt. She looked like she belonged on a farm.

They got settled in the cafeteria and spent some time getting to know each other. Amy did live on a small farm and had two cows, a pig, and chickens. She only lived 20 minutes away from the school, but it was on the outskirts of the suburbs. Miriam told her about her parents and that she lived with her grandma. She also told her about her aunt and uncle being in Kenya, helping at an orphanage. Amy mentioned that she had heard of the orphanage from her brother, who was in seventh grade this year. Then, they got to work reviewing the last chapter Miriam's teacher had taught before Christmas break. They spent a few minutes doing some of the homework problems for the night. By the time their session was done, Miriam felt Amy was a good fit to help her bring her math grade up. She thanked Amy, and they planned to do another session next week. Miriam met her grandma outside the high school at 4:30 p.m.

"How did it go?" she asked.

"Great! My tutor is named Amy, and she's really nice. She lives on a farm," Miriam said.

"Was she helpful with math?"

"Very much so. I should be able to finish tonight's homework very easily. Amy explained things really well," Miriam told her.

"Good, good," Grandma said.

Miriam worked very hard that third quarter to bring her grades up. Grandma noticed and told Miriam that if her grades were up, which meant all A's and B's, they could get tickets to the new musical showing downtown. Miriam loved going to the theater.

Thursday was the last day of school before spring break, and Miriam was very nervous when she was handed her report card at the end of the day. She had been checking on her grades every week, and they had all been good — but she had thought that last quarter, and it hadn't ended well. Miriam opened the envelope and saw only one B among the A's. The B was in science, but they had been covering dinosaurs, and she had a hard time keeping all of them straight. She smiled and looked over at Steph. They both gave each other a thumbs-up this time, and Steph gave Miriam a big smile. She mouthed, "Good job!" Miriam just stared at her report card, smiling, until the bell rang. She would get to go to the theater this week!

Miriam asked Grandma if she could still tutor with Amy in the fourth quarter to see if she could bring her science grade up, too. Grandma had no problem with that, and neither did Amy. Amy loved science almost as much as she loved math. The fourth quarter was spent learning about space, and Amy even helped Miriam study for math when she had quizzes and tests coming up. Toward the end of the year, Miriam's grades were all solid A's. If she did well on her finals, she would get all A's on her report card.

Miriam wanted to thank Amy for helping her, so she asked her grandma to take her shopping. Amy collected panda items, and, at the local bookstore, Miriam found a panda journal, bookmark, pencil, and mug. She gave them to Amy at their last session.

"Guess you won't be needing my help next year," Amy said. "You've got some really good study skills now, and you're very smart on your own."

"I'm so glad you were able to help me, though," Miriam replied. "Maybe I can help tutor kids when I'm a junior or senior, too."

"Now, that would make me really happy," Amy told her. "It's always good to help others when you can."

Amy gave Miriam a hug.

"Have a great summer, and I'll see you around next year," Amy said. "Remember to call me and let me know your final grades, though."

Her friends were going to have their typical end-of-school-year sleepover at Sydney's house again, but they knew it was dependent on what they all got for their final grades. They met at Miriam's locker right after the bell rang at the end of the day.

"I got all A's!" Miriam told them excitedly.

"Me, too," Steph responded.

"I got two B's, but my mom is happy with those," Anna said.

All the others got grades their parents would be happy with.

"The End of Freshman Year party is on!" Sydney said. "See you all in just a few hours!"

That night, they talked about the school year and looked through the yearbook. They took turns signing each other's yearbooks and talking about summer plans. Grandma was going to take her on a road trip for two weeks this summer to see some of America's landmarks, but she wouldn't tell Miriam exactly where yet. Steph's family was going to Florida, and Sydney's family was going to Hawaii. Karen was going on a cruise to Alaska — they all asked if they could stow away for that trip. Michelle, Grace, and Anna all had family reunions in different states.

"Does anyone know any good places to get a job this summer?" Miriam asked. "Grandma wants me to help pay for part of my car."

Most of her friends would be given a car when they turned 16 — maybe not a brand new one, but their parents saw a car as a rite of passage. Grandma said having a car was not something that automatically happened in their family. Miriam had been saving up for a couple of years, but just from birthday and babysitting money. She had $2,712 saved up, and Grandma would match her dollar for dollar.

"Would you want to lifeguard at the pool?" Karen asked.

"I think you can do that or help as a day camp counselor at the community center when you're 15," Michelle offered. "Most other places, like stores and restaurants, want you to be 16."

"Lifeguarding could be fun. I'll have Grandma ask what training that involves."

"Sorry you have to work," Steph said. "But, if you're a lifeguard, I could probably come to the pool and hang out with you."

"Yeah, we all could," Sydney agreed.

"That would make it more fun," Miriam said. "I'll keep you guys posted on what I do."

Miriam's grandma thought working as a lifeguard was an excellent idea. She took Miriam with her to the community center the next time she went and had Miriam talk to the director about what was required. Miriam was given the study guide and told to come on Friday at 10 a.m. for a written test, swimming test, and hands-on training. It would last for four hours, and she would need to bring her own lunch. Miriam could work up to 20 hours a week, and the pay was decent.

Grandma planned the road trip for the end of the summer, so Miriam could work until the last three weeks of vacation. The director was fine with that but also mentioned that they could use lifeguards all through the year, so if Miriam liked it, she could still work some hours after school started back up.

Miriam had always loved to swim, so she was very excited to see the lifeguard job opportunity coming together. Her friends were happy, too. Steph told her they should celebrate when she passed all the tests and was officially hired.

Miriam read the study guide from cover to cover each day before the Friday test. She felt confident while taking the test and found the swimming test just as easy. There were three other teens there, but Miriam only recognized one from school. Charlie was in her math class. The other two were girls and said they were homeschooled. The hands-on training had them rescue each other from the pool, practice CPR on a dummy, and throw out the flotation devices to each other and drag each other to the side of the pool. The two girls were already friends, so Miriam and Charlie paired up for the training.

"Are you working for a car, too?" Charlie asked her as they were waiting for the girls to finish the flotation device training.

"Yep, my grandma is making me work for it," Miriam said. She had pulled her curls back up into a high ponytail for the day.

"My parents make me work for everything I want," Charlie complained, running his fingers through his black hair. "I have to give them gas money for them to bring me here. They say I have 'buy-in' if I have to work for it."

"Wow, I guess I don't have it so bad then," Miriam grinned.

"Okay, Charlie and Miriam, you're up," the director called to them.

All four of the teens were hired at the end of the training. Miriam's first shift would be the next day. She would work for four hours each Saturday and Sunday afternoon and then Tuesdays, Wednesdays, and Thursdays in the morning during swim lessons. Charlie would work with her on Saturdays, Wednesdays, and Thursdays.

When she told Michelle and Anna that night at their Friday get-together, Anna told Miriam that Charlie was her next-door neighbor. They were at Miriam's house that night since only the three of them were in town. The group had decided to keep up the Friday night tradition during the summer with whoever was in town.

"He seems really nice," Miriam said. "He was in my math class last year, but that's the first time I'd been around him. He was pretty quiet in class."

"He plays soccer," Michelle told her. "I've seen him out there when we practice. We played together in third and fourth grade when it was co-ed."

"You said you guys work together tomorrow? Maybe we should go swimming tomorrow," Anna said. Anna was turning into the girl in their group who was most interested in boys. She had told them she was determined to have a boyfriend next year. Miriam didn't really want the distraction of a boyfriend yet.

Anna and Michelle did come to the community center to swim the next day. However, Charlie and Miriam were actually so busy with their job that they didn't get much time to socialize at all. They could talk during the 10-minute break at the end of the hour when it wasn't Miriam's turn to keep an eye on the adults swimming, but Miriam found she really needed to focus on the people in the pool. She almost dove in once when she glanced over and saw a toddler's head go underwater, but then the mom pulled her right back up. The mom was holding the little girl and letting her bob up and down to blow bubbles. Miriam hoped she wouldn't have to rescue anyone while she was working. Still, after seeing the toddler, it sunk in how much responsibility she had with the job.

Miriam managed to save up another $1,000 before it was time to go on the road trip with Grandma. A few days before they left, Grandma finally sat Miriam down to tell her where they would be going.

"We're going to visit the Wizard of Oz Museum, the Little House on the Prairie Museum, Denver, Salt Lake City, the Grand Canyon, Albuquerque, and Oklahoma City. I've found some really interesting historical stops along the way, too," she said.

"Wow, Grandma, that's a lot of places!" Miriam exclaimed.

"I want to show you some of the country before you get really busy working. I actually took your mom and aunt on a similar adventure when they were 16 and 14," Grandma said. "I'll tell you some of their stories along the way.

"Make sure to pack at least five outfits and your swimsuit. You'll want good walking shoes and flip-flops. Pack one summer dress in case we find a nice restaurant along the way. I'll grab us some audiobooks at the library tomorrow."

"I'm excited!" Miriam exclaimed. "This will be an adventure."

Grandma woke Miriam up early the morning they were leaving, and Miriam found two presents on the kitchen table.

"These are early birthday presents from Uncle Mike and Aunt Susan," Grandma said. "I told them about the trip months ago, and they really wanted you to have these before you left."

Miriam unwrapped them to find a travel journal that looked like a passport and a digital camera. The card with it said they wanted her to be able to look back on her trip whenever she wanted and that they couldn't wait to see all the photos she took during the journey.

"These are really thoughtful," Miriam said. "Can I email them really quick before we get on the road?"

"That sounds like a good idea, but eat first so I can wash these dishes up. We'll leave in 30 minutes," Grandma responded.

Miriam ate, emailed her aunt and uncle, got dressed, and packed up her last-minute toiletries. She put the camera and journal in her backpack, which mostly contained books to read during the trip. She brought her bags downstairs and helped Grandma load them and a cooler of food into the car. Then, they were off.

Miriam wrote in her journal several times a day, documenting each part of the trip. She tracked state license plates in the back cover. Miriam's favorite part of the trip was seeing the Grand Canyon. They stayed to watch the sun set that day, and Miriam took so many pictures, they had to buy a new storage card for the camera the next day. Grandma told her a lot of stories about what her mom and aunt did when they went on the trip with her and Grandpa. Miriam often felt like this trip was something she would have done with her grandma even if her parents were still alive. She loved that Grandma would talk about them so often.

When they finally got back home, it was already dark. They simply unpacked what they needed and were both in bed within an hour. There was nothing like sleeping in your own bed, Miriam thought as she looked around her room before closing her eyes. The attic door that led to Orphan Wish Island, the window seat, the picture of her parents, and her bed all meant that she was home.

Chapter 11

Instead of orientation, sophomores, juniors, and seniors just had an afternoon where they could stop by the school and pick up their schedules. They had requested their classes at the end of their previous year. When they compared schedules on the last Friday night of summer, they were all pretty satisfied with how many classes they had together.

In choir, they learned that they would be able to try out for show choir and the a cappella group the week before Christmas break. For the first semester, they would stay in the general choir, then in the second semester, they would join the other choir to practice before trying out. Based on tryouts, they would stay with the other choir or come back to the general choir.

"I really want to try out for show choir," Miriam told her friends at lunch. "Their performance last spring was so impressive. I heard they travel and do performances in the area as well."

"I'm sticking with the general choir," Steph told her. "I like my voice to blend in with the crowd."

"I'm with you, Steph," Anna agreed.

"I started voice lessons over the summer," Sydney announced. "I'm going to be brave and try out for the a cappella group."

"Wow, Sydney, that is brave," Miriam said. "Do you like your voice teacher?"

"Yes, she's very nice. I think my mom actually got the recommendation from your grandma. It's Mrs. Wilson from your church," Sydney remarked.

"Oh, she's really nice," Miriam told her. "She helps in the nursery with me some Sundays."

Michelle came over just then and sat down.

"I did it, guys! I made the varsity soccer team!" she said.

They all congratulated her, and the talk turned to sports and boys. There was a fall dance coming up at the beginning of October, but Miriam planned to see if she could work that night. Her friends were going as a group, but Miriam didn't feel like getting dressed up just to hang out and talk. Steph, Michelle, and Anna were all holding out the hope that a boy would ask them to go, and if that happened, then the whole group wouldn't be going together anyway.

Miriam's regular lifeguarding schedule was Mondays after school and Saturday mornings. She had piano on Wednesdays after school, and there was Kindness Club every other Friday. She started good study habits early in the year and had a good set of grades by the time the dance rolled around. Steph and Anna were both asked to go with boys, and they accepted. When Miriam asked if she could work that Friday night, the director was happy and relieved, as two of the people she had tried to schedule had already asked for that night off. The two girls who had trained at the same time had decided they didn't want to lifeguard anymore, so the director had more slots to fill. Miriam could work every Friday after school if she wanted. Miriam told the director she would have to check with her grandmother but that she probably could. That would bring her hours up to 10 hours a week — three each day after school and four on Saturday morning. With that, she would be able to help with some of her car insurance and have gas money.

Miriam was anxiously waiting for her birthday that year. She knew her wish, but she also knew Grandma would take her car shopping as soon as she got her driver's license. Miriam was going to take the test after school on her birthday, which was on a Thursday. If she passed, they would go car shopping on the weekend. She didn't want to miss the door to the island opening that night. Her friends planned to celebrate her birthday on their Friday get together later in the month. They were all much busier this year, so instead of meeting every Friday, they changed it to the last Friday of the month. They had all committed to try their hardest to keep that one night a month free so they could have their time together. They were going to forgo the Halloween party this year and just have a sleepover at Sydney's with just them.

Miriam's grandma picked her up after school on her birthday. They waited for the parking lot to clear, then she let Miriam drive to the testing station. She had been letting her drive them home from the community center after lifeguarding since school started. Miriam was nervous but fairly confident that she would pass her test. They filled out the paperwork, and Miriam took the written test, which was actually on a computer. She only got one question wrong, which was how much distance to allow when following a motorcycle. Miriam had thought you gave them more room, but it was the same as following a car. Grandma congratulated her, gave her a kiss on her head, and then wished her luck for the driving test. The test-giver told her to drive up to the high school and park. He didn't say much else but noted things on his clipboard as she drove. She parked at the school and looked to him to see what to do next.

"Well, you didn't stop for five complete seconds at the last stop sign, and you forgot to signal as we left the testing station parking lot, but everything else is fine so far. I want you to back out of this spot, drive back to the testing station, and park in the No. 3 spot," he told Miriam. Miriam took a deep breath and did exactly as he asked.

When they got back to the testing station, he just told Miriam to go back inside to wait for her results. He didn't smile, so she couldn't tell how well she did.

"How did you do?" Grandma asked her when she sat back down next to her.

"I think I did well, but the man didn't say," Miriam said. "He said I didn't stop long enough at a stop sign and forgot my turn signal once, but that's all he said."

"I'm sure you did fine," Grandma said. "If you're doing really bad, they have you pull over, and they take over the driving."

"Miriam Stanley, please come to Window 3," a voice said over the speaker. Grandma walked over with Miriam. A lady with her brown hair up in a bun smiled at Miriam as she approached the window.

"Congratulations, Miriam, you are now a licensed driver!" the lady said.

Miriam's smile stretched across her face. Grandma gave her a hug. "Thank you!" Miriam said.

Miriam kept staring at her license as they walked out to the car.

"Want to drive us out to dinner?" Grandma asked. "We need to celebrate both your birthday and your driver's license."

"Yes!" Miriam exclaimed.

"Guess we're going car shopping after you finish lifeguarding on Saturday," Grandma said. "I'm very happy for you, Miriam. Happy birthday!"

Miriam was thinking about what color car she really wanted when the street lamps finally started flickering. She hopped off the window seat and headed for the attic door. She stopped in front of it for a moment and read over the words. After today, she would only visit the island two more times — once for her final wish and once to hear her parents' wishes and message. She knew what she wanted to wish for tonight. It would make her year very fun.

Miriam took a deep breath of the ocean scent as she stepped through the door. Like every year, there was a slight breeze that gently moved her hair as she shut the attic door. She slowly walked toward the big Starfruit tree, not seeing anyone else on the island at first. As she got closer, she saw Lexi sitting against the tree, talking to Stella, who was sitting on a branch of the tree just above Lexi.

"We decided to wait for you," Lexi told Miriam. "I told Stella there was no way you wouldn't show up."

"You were right," Stella said to Lexi. "Time will tell if Amelia comes back this year. I'm glad you two have committed to coming to the island each year. Ready to make your wishes?"

Lexi hopped up and went straight to her Starfruit. Miriam had to look halfway around the tree before she found hers.

Like the year before, Miriam found a spot away from the tree to sit by herself. She held the Starfruit for a while, thinking about all the things she wished she could tell her parents.

Mom and Dad, I passed my driver's test and will go car shopping tomorrow, Miriam said to them in her head. *Grandma's great, but I wish you had been here to teach me how to drive. I've been getting good grades and have good friends. I am going to wish to make it into the show choir this year. I think you'd have loved to see me perform. I miss you.*

Miriam then took a bite, wished to make it into the show choir, and listened intently to her parents' message. She smiled as they called her Miribug. Grandma didn't call her that much anymore, since she was getting older. Miriam sat there for a while, just replaying the message in her head before she got up to bury her Starfruit.

"You sat there for a very long time," Stella commented as she came over to Miriam. "Lexi has already left. I don't think Amelia is coming this year."

"I realized I only have two more visits after today," Miriam said. "I wanted to take my time listening to my parents' message, and remembering them."

Stella put her hand on Miriam's shoulder. "They are always with you," Stella said. "It's the ones who are loved the most that usually come to the island year after year. Love draws them to their parents."

"I feel like I should miss them more sometimes, but it's been eight years now since they died," Miriam confessed. "I think about them often, but life is sometimes so busy that there are days I barely look at their photo before going to bed."

"Oh, Miriam, they know, and they don't expect you to dwell on how much you miss them. All parents want their children to live full lives. I've heard that many times from the children who come all the years — their parents told them to live their lives to the fullest."

"I am trying to do that," Miriam said. "This year will be the year of show choir and driving and starting to think about college."

"Sounds wonderful," Stella told her. They were standing in front of Miriam's door now. "Enjoy your year." Then Stella flew back toward the tree in the middle of the island.

"Bye," Miriam said and walked back into her bedroom. She almost didn't open the attic door back up, but she couldn't help herself. She always held out a small glimmer of hope that the island would be there, but it was just the attic and boxes again.

She got into bed and stared at her parents' picture until she fell asleep.

Miriam was in a very good mood the next morning and started singing as she got breakfast ready. This year, Grandma was sleeping in a little later, so Miriam offered to start making breakfast for them. It was still always eggs and toast, but she thanked Miriam every morning when she came into the kitchen.

"Must have been a good visit to the island last night," Grandma remarked as she sat down at the table to eat.

"It was, although I realized I only have two visits left," Miriam admitted. "I wished for something very fun for this year. I'll let you know when it happens."

"Sounds good, Miriam. Thank you for breakfast again. I don't know why I'm more tired these past few months," Grandma said.

"We all need different amounts of sleep at different ages," Miriam remarked. "I'm happy to make you breakfast. You've definitely made it for me often enough."

The next day, after her lifeguarding shift, Miriam's grandma took her car shopping. Grandma knew someone from church who worked at a used car dealership, and they had headed there right after Miriam's lifeguard session. They had driven three cars and settled on a navy blue car that ended up being $1,000 less than Miriam could afford. She felt like a millionaire, having both a car and money still in her savings account.

Chapter 12

A few weeks later, Mr. Nuskett announced it was time to move to the other choirs if they planned to try out for those choirs in a few weeks. Only Sydney and one other girl planned to try out for the a cappella choir. Six students, including Miriam, were going to try out for the show choir. Mr. Nuskett made it clear that not everyone who tried out for the special choirs made it in, but that everyone in the regular choir had great talent, too. He said there was no set number of students for any of the choirs; they just had to do their best in whatever group they were singing with.

Miriam's first day in show choir left her head spinning. There were no chairs in the room — the choir stood for the entire class to help build up their stamina. They not only had to learn their singing parts and memorize them, but they also had to learn and memorize the choreography that went along with each song. They all had to sing a few basic lines so Mr. Nuskett could place them in the right singing section. Miriam was put with the second sopranos — they often sang the melody, but if there were any harmony parts for the sopranos, it would default to them. They sang the lower soprano notes. Miriam had been a second soprano in the regular choir, too, so she wasn't surprised.

After the new students were placed in their singing parts, Mr. Nuskett dove right into a song. The rest of the show choir knew it already, and the six new students did their best to keep up. After singing the song three times, they were asked to step to the side so they could see the movements. Then, they joined the choir for the movements and tried their best to keep up. At the end of class, Mr. Nuskett asked them to practice at home, as this would be their tryout song in three weeks. When it was over, Miriam was sweating about as much as she did at the end of gym class.

By the end of the first week, two of the students had decided not to try out but to go back to the regular choir. Miriam and the other three girls talked after class that Friday about getting together to practice. Angela and Kristy were altos, but Cassidy was a second soprano, too. None of their after-school schedules matched, so they planned to get together during lunch at least three times a week. They decided on Mondays, Wednesdays, and Thursdays. Miriam decided it would be worth missing Kindness Club to practice for her show choir audition.

Miriam told her friends about her lunch plans that Friday night at their monthly get-together. She had stopped spending the night on the weekends when she had lifeguard duty. She didn't want to be tired on her shift, which started at 8 a.m. She was glad she had the job. She needed the money for gas and insurance and was starting to save up for college. Shortly after her 16th birthday, her grandma had sat her down and told her that her parents had left her a trust that she could use for college, but she would have to pay for half of the tuition, and the trust would match it. The trust would also cover books, room and board for two years on campus, and two years on- or off-campus. Then, upon graduation, she could take control of the remainder of the trust. It was a very bittersweet talk for both of them. There was some relief that there was money for college, but she would rather have her parents back in a heartbeat. Miriam could tell Grandma felt the same way.

For the next two weeks, unless Miriam was in class, at work, or sleeping, she was working on her show choir audition song. She had found the sheet music and even spent her piano practice time playing and singing the song. She hummed it while getting ready in the morning and going to bed at night. She felt like she was going to wear a hole in the rug in her room from practicing the dance steps. Mr. Nuskett had given them all a CD with the music on it — both with singing and without singing — so they could practice at home. When audition day came, Miriam felt a little nervous but very confident. They had been told early on that it would be a solo audition in front of the whole class. Miriam planned to offer to go first to get the ordeal over with, but Cassidy beat her to it. Miriam would go second, then Angela and Krystal.

Cassidy had the singing down pat, but messed up a few of the dance moves. The class was very supportive, though, and gave her a loud, long round of applause when she was done. They had all been up there in front of the class at one point and remembered what it was like.

It took a few minutes to cue the music back up before Miriam's turn. She closed her eyes and took some deep breaths.

"Oh, Miriam, we love you so much!" she heard her mother's voice in her head. She opened her eyes and smiled, and the music started ...

Miriam nailed every part of the routine except being slow on one turn. She quickly got back on track. She even took a little bow at the end. The whole class clapped loud and long for her, too. She glanced at Mr. Nuskett as she walked back over to her seat and saw that he was smiling. *I might just make it*, Miriam thought.

Angela and Krystal both did very well on their tryouts, too. Miriam thought they all four had a good shot of making the choir, but they would have to wait until Monday to find out. The list would be posted before school on Monday morning, and the students that made it would join the choir for the last week of the second quarter before winter break.

Miriam tried to keep herself distracted that weekend. She got called early Saturday to take an extra lifeguarding shift since another lifeguard called in sick. Then, she invited Steph over for a movie on Saturday night, worked on homework, and read. She tried practicing piano on Sunday, but she kept thinking about her audition and whether it had been good enough. She gave up after 10 minutes and went to her room to read. After dinner, she sent her weekly emails to her aunt, uncle, and pen pal then went to bed early, willing Monday to come.

Miriam left for school 15 minutes early. Her grandma was just waking up as she walked out the door.

"Your breakfast is staying warm in the oven," Miriam told her. "I've got to go see if I made show choir."

"Thank you, Miriam. Have a good day! Whatever happens, I think you're the best singer around. Love you!"

When Miriam got to the choir door, she saw Cassidy was already there.

"He hasn't posted it yet," Cassidy told Miriam as she walked up. "But he just got here a minute ago, so he should be back out with the list in a minute."

"Thanks," Miriam replied. The door opened, and Mr. Nuskett smiled at them and taped a list to the door. Then, he walked back into the classroom. They both walked up to the door quickly and scoured for their names.

"Yes, we all made it!" Miriam cried.

"Shh, here come Angela and Krystal — let them find out for themselves," Cassidy said.

Miriam and Cassidy stood back and let Angela and Krystal read the list. They shouted and hugged and then ran over to Miriam and Cassidy. Then, all four of the girls hugged.

"This is awesome!" Krystal exclaimed. "I'm so glad we all made it!"

"Me, too!" Angela agreed. "We'll have to celebrate. Let's all meet up at lunch."

"Sounds good," Miriam said. "It's going to be a fun second semester."

"Not just that, it'll be a fun time for the rest of high school — show choir is so elite, and we're in it," Cassidy chimed in.

Outside first class, both Sydney and Karen were anxiously awaiting her arrival to find out if she made it into the show choir. Before they could even ask, she spilled the news.

"I made it in!" Miriam cried. "Did you get into a cappella choir, Sydney?"

"I did! It's so exciting!" exclaimed Sydney.

"I'll tell the others when I see them in classes this morning," Karen told them. "It's time for a celebration! I baked cookies to share at lunch, just in case."

"Thank you, Karen," said Sydney.

"I'm actually eating lunch with the other show choir girls who made it in today," Miriam answered.

"Oh," Sydney said. "Well, maybe tomorrow ..."

The bell rang, and they had to get themselves into the classroom. Miriam felt bad since she hadn't eaten with her friends in a few weeks, but she wanted to celebrate with her show choir friends, too. She'd make it up to her friends somehow. *Maybe I can start taking us all out for lunch once a week after winter break since they're going to try having an open campus for lunch for a while*, Miriam thought. She would make room for all of her friends.

"Before Mr. Nuskett comes in, can I talk to everyone for a minute?" Julie spoke loudly in the show choir room. She was a senior who had straight blond hair that went down to her waist, and she always wore it down.

"Show choir is a unique group," she began once everyone turned their attention to her. "We have to not only sing in harmony but dance as one solid group. A few weeks before school gets out for summer, we are planning to enter the statewide choir contest. We don't do this every year, but Mr. Nuskett asked the PTO to sponsor us this year, and they said yes. For us seniors, we would love nothing more than to get first place. In order to do that, we all need to work really hard for the rest of the school year. I will plan two after-school sessions for practice every week, starting the week after we get back after winter break. You need to attend at least one of them. Also, as much as you can, I would like us to start eating lunch in this room so we can work on singing and bond as a choir. I promise it won't just be all work — we'll have some fun, too."

The bell rang, and Mr. Nuskett walked into the room.

"Just let me know if you have any questions," Julie said and then turned to Mr. Nuskett. "I was telling them about the state choir competition."

"Oh, good. It's going to be exciting. Bristolway hasn't competed in five years," Mr. Nuskett told the class. "We'll need three songs to perform. I have an idea for one, which we'll work on a little this week, and then I'll decide for sure which three songs we'll use over winter break so we can get to work on them right away when we come back to school. Let's get started on our warm-ups."

Miriam was excited, but then she remembered her idea about taking her friends out to lunch. She'd have to find some way to make it work. She could surely miss one lunch period a week. Piano, show choir, lifeguarding, and Kindness Club — life was going to be busy.

Miriam did eat lunch with her friends the next day, but in show choir, Cassidy asked why she hadn't shown up for lunch in the choir room. She was the only person missing besides two people who were sick.

"I didn't realize the lunch thing started this week," Miriam said.

"It does, and the look on Julie's face wasn't good when she took attendance and you were missing," Cassidy said. "I told her you just probably forgot. You need to come tomorrow."

"Okay, I will. Thanks for covering for me," Miriam replied.

Miriam spent the rest of her lunches that week in the show choir room. It was a fun time, as the show choir members were all very friendly and outgoing. There was a lot of eating, joking, and singing each lunch period. Miriam sat with Cassidy, Angela, and Krystal, but often two or three of the older members sat with them, too. They all got invited to two parties over winter break. Miriam knew she could go to both since she and Grandma weren't traveling for the holidays. Krystal was going to Ohio, but Cassidy and Angela planned to go to the parties, too. One was on Friday night to celebrate school getting out, and the other was for New Year's Eve. Miriam was glad her other friends hadn't been able to have their regular Friday night get-together that week. Since Christmas was Tuesday, everyone but Anna and her were heading out of town right after school on Friday or early Saturday morning. They'd get together right before school started up again. She missed them, but she didn't want to have to choose between her new friends and her old friends.

Miriam enjoyed both parties over winter break. The show choir get-together was a lot of eating, singing, and dancing. They did a few trust activities that Julie suggested would make them work better together. With her friends, Miriam watched a movie and talked about school, how breaks went — and boys. For Christmas, Miriam got a few gift cards to get some new clothing. That was all she really wanted. She got Grandma some kitchen towels, utensils, and a cutting board since the old ones were all worn out. She sent her aunt and uncle some of her savings to spend however they wanted at the orphanage for Christmas. They emailed her to let her know they had used it to throw a little party, where every child got a notebook, coloring pencils, and some candy. Miriam could tell it was a big hit from the pictures they sent.

In show choir, it was announced that after-school practices would be on Wednesdays and Fridays. She didn't want to give up her piano lessons on Wednesday, and she sometimes had lifeguarding on Friday. However, she could do that on Saturdays and Sundays instead, and it would be over before she met up with her friends once a month. Cassidy and Krystal would be going on Fridays, too. Angela had a family commitment on Fridays, so she would be going to the Wednesday practice.

At the first Friday practice, Miriam left as they were ordering pizza. It had been a good rehearsal. They were starting by getting the singing down for all three songs. Miriam didn't know they would be having dinner, but it seemed that they switched from rehearsal to a get-together around dinnertime. Miriam knew Grandma was expecting her for dinner, but she could plan to stay for the rest of the Fridays.

Two weeks later, Sydney reminded her in homeroom about getting together that night at her house.

"We really miss you at lunch," Sydney said.

"I miss you guys, too," Miriam confided. "This show choir competition is going to be a neat opportunity, but it is going to take a lot of time this semester. It usually isn't like this."

"I hope not!" Sydney replied. "You're missing some good stuff — like Karen got asked to the Spring Fling dance by Jeremy!"

"What? She's got to be so happy. She's only been eyeing him since the first day of school," Miriam laughed. "Tell her I said I'm so happy for her!"

"No, you can tell her tonight — right?" Sydney asked.

"Right. I'll do it then. I can't wait to catch up with you all tonight. What movie are we watching?"

"I thought we could watch the new Puppy Island movie. I know it's animated, but it's really, really funny," Sydney said.

"I haven't seen that one yet," Miriam told her as the bell rang.

Miriam fully intended to join her friends that night, but they started rehearsing some of the dance moves of one of the songs during practice, and it ran long. When the pizzas arrived, they just took a quick break, then Julie wanted to show them some of the moves from the other two songs, so they had a basic idea before they did them in class next week. When they finally finished, Miriam chatted with Cassidy and Krystal for a few minutes, and then she was ready to leave. She hoped Grandma wouldn't be asleep when she got home.

"Who's there?" Grandma asked as Miriam opened the door. "Everything okay, dear?"

"Yes, show choir practice just ran long."

"Aren't you supposed to be with your friends tonight?"

"Oh, no! I totally forgot. Can I go see if they're still there? They were going to watch a movie, but it wasn't a sleepover night."

"Sure," Grandma replied. Miriam opened the front door and saw Steph walking back into her house. Steph never left until everyone else had left. Miriam closed the door back up. She would have to call Sydney in the morning and apologize — after her lifeguarding duty.

"They've already all gone home. I saw Steph go into her house," Miriam told her. "I can't believe I forgot about it. I already hardly see them at all during the week."

"I'm sure they'll understand," Grandma told her.

"I hope so," Miriam replied, but she was started to not feel as close to them as she once had.

Miriam tried calling both Steph and Sydney before heading to lifeguarding Saturday morning, but neither answered the phone. She had to force herself to stay focused while she was lifeguarding. She was worried that her friends would be upset with her. Luckily, it was just a swimming class for seniors and adult lap swim while she was on duty, which didn't require the same focus as when children were at the pool. She tried calling her friends again when she got home, but they still didn't answer, so she worked on her homework and practiced piano. The phone finally rang after dinner; it was Steph.

"So, where were you last night? Is everything okay? I saw your car at the house when I came home," Steph said.

"I just totally spaced," Miriam answered. "We were practicing for show choir, and I got sidetracked and lost track of time. By the time I left, I had forgotten about getting together with you guys. As soon as I realized what I had done, I went to see if you guys were still hanging out, but I saw you had just come home. I'm so sorry."

"Sydney was really bummed you missed it," Steph told her. "She said she hardly sees you at all anymore."

"I know — between work, school, and show choir, I barely have enough time for anything else. But I miss seeing you guys."

"Well, we decided to have a surprise party for Karen next month, so make sure you can come to that. Sydney's mom is going to buy canvases so we can do one of those painting sessions. I think we're going to paint a koala."

"That sounds awesome. I will be there for sure! Thanks for calling me back. Can I take you all out to lunch on Monday to make up for it?"

"I bet that would work. I'll pass the word along Monday morning."

"Thanks."

"Talk to you later. Bye."

"Bye."

Miriam felt a little relieved that at least one of her friends was willing to talk to her. She would try Sydney again tomorrow, and if she didn't get through, she would show up early on Monday to speak to her.

Miriam spent most of Sunday working on an English essay and getting ahead on homework for the week. The phone didn't ring at all. She took a break and watched a movie with Grandma before heading to bed. She could tell Grandma was hoping she would talk with her about what was going on, but Miriam didn't want to talk with her about how she had hurt her friends.

"Sydney! Sydney! Wait up!" Miriam shouted to her friend as she jogged into school. Sydney slowed down a little but didn't stop completely. Miriam caught up with her, and Sydney finally stopped.

"Sydney, I am so sorry I didn't make it Friday night. I honestly forgot about it while I was at show choir. I shouldn't have. I promise I won't make that mistake again."

"Are you sure? Because if you want to just ditch us and have your new show choir friends, you can do that." Sydney began to walk away.

"No. Show choir is fun, but you guys are more important than singing. This is just temporary, and it's crazier than normal because of the competition this spring."

"I hope you mean that."

"I do. Let me take you all off-campus for lunch today. Steph also told me about the thing going on next month. I won't miss it!"

"Okay — I guess we all make mistakes. I'll definitely let you take me out to lunch — milkshakes are on you!"

They were almost to the door to the classroom at this point. They hugged and went in just as the bell rang.

Miriam made it a point to take her friends off campus for lunch every Monday in February and planned to do it for the rest of the year. She always felt happier after spending time with them. They had also started emailing each other more to plan the details for Karen's surprise party. Miriam volunteered to be in charge of the cake. Her Grandma knew how to do all kinds of designs with frosting, and Miriam was going to ask her to help make a cake that looked like a stack of books. They made the cake the day before the party, and it looked really neat. Grandma had skipped her walking group to help Miriam decorate it, and Miriam would stop by after show choir practice to pick up the cake and her sleepover bag before heading to Sydney's house.

The afternoon of Karen's party, Miriam glanced at the clock every few minutes. She was not going to be late tonight. They had a good practice and had almost all the moves down for the two songs. They would start practicing on the stage next week. Julie seemed pleased by their progress and was taking their practices for the competition very seriously. The pizzas arrived just as Julie was saying they would stop for the night. It was 5:30 p.m., and Miriam was planning to be at Sydney's by 7 p.m. She had time to grab a quick bite and then head home.

"You have a car, right?" Cassidy asked Miriam as she grabbed a slice of pepperoni pizza after Miriam.

"I do. Why?" Miriam asked.

"Krystal and I were supposed to go home with Angela and then head to the movies, but her parents are sick," Cassidy said. "My dad is working tonight, and we only have one car. Krystal can't get her parents to answer. Is there any way you can take us all to Angela's house, then we can wait for our parents there?"

"Where does Angela live?" Miriam asked.

"About five minutes from here by the Sunset gas station," Cassidy said.

"That's on my way home, but I'm not supposed to have passengers until this summer," Miriam told her.

"Please, Miriam! It would take us more than 30 minutes to walk, and it's starting to get dark. We won't tell anyone," Cassidy said.

"Okay, but we need to leave in 10 minutes," Miriam said. She was uneasy, but she felt she should help her friends out. It was just a short drive, and then Miriam could get ready for Karen's party.

Her friends were ready to go in 10 minutes. Cassidy sat in the passenger seat, while Angela and Krystal sat in the back. Cassidy immediately started playing with the radio station setting after buckling up.

"Check PopRocks, Cassidy," Angela said. "I think it's 101.7. They always have the most recent music on."

Miriam concentrated on driving and pulled out of the school parking lot. She turned left to head down the school road, then it would be another left on Main Street to get to the gas station.

"Let me know where to turn when we get close to your house, Angela," Miriam said. As she was turning onto Main Street, the two girls in the back told Cassidy to turn up the music. It was the newest hit from Jeremiah, and they all started singing to it. Cassidy began to dance a bit in her seat. Miriam smiled and sang, too. As they got close to the gas station, the song was coming to an end, and Miriam reached over to turn the volume down. Cassidy must have thought she was reaching out to hold hands to dance along. Miriam tried to pull her hand back to find the volume control, but before she could, Cassidy pulled her toward her a bit. Miriam leaned back toward her side of the car but moved the steering wheel at the same time. She heard screams and the loud crunch of metal and then nothing.

Miriam woke up in the hospital and saw Grandma sitting in a chair nearby. She had her eyes closed. Miriam felt sore all over, but her left leg felt painful and heavy. She could feel a bandage on her forehead as well. Oh no! She must have been in an accident when she had Cassidy, Angela, and Krystal in her car. She was going to be in trouble. She had to know if her friends were okay.

"Grandma?" Miriam said weakly. Her grandmother didn't stir. She said it louder.

"Miri, you're awake," Grandma said as she stood up and moved to the side of Miriam's bed. She grabbed Miriam's hand and squeezed it gently. "You've been out for almost two days. Do you remember what happened?"

Miriam hung her head. She couldn't look her in the eyes. "Somewhat. I was in a car accident and had friends in the car with me. Are they okay?"

"Yes, they are, and that is what happened. You were the only one with serious injuries. The rest, including the truck driver you hit, just had bumps and bruises," she assured Miriam.

"I hit a truck?" Miriam asked in disbelief. She hadn't even seen it on the road.

"Yes, and that's why the truck driver is okay, and you have a broken leg."

"A broken leg?" Miriam finally looked down at her body and saw a cast barely sticking out of the end of the sheet on her left leg. That's why it felt heavy. Miriam started crying. So much had changed for her in just a few seconds.

"It'll be okay, Miriam," Grandma said, reaching out to touch her hand. "There are some consequences, but everyone is still alive, and that's something to be grateful for."

"Consequences?" Miriam asked through her tears. "I know I can't do show choir with a broken leg, but what else? Oh... I won't be able to drive for a while, even after my leg heals, right?"

"Most likely. We actually have to go to court in a few months to determine what consequences affect your driving. The car is totaled, too."

Miriam didn't say anything but just thought about what her Grandma said. All those hours spent lifeguarding so she could buy a car, and she messed it up by simply not following the rules. She could only be mad at herself. So much for her wish this year, too. She made show choir but wouldn't be able to participate anymore.

"Are you hungry?" Grandma asked. "I can get you something from the cafeteria."

"I am, a little bit," Miriam said, still sniffling.

"Okay, I'll be back shortly. Just try to rest. The doctor said you would need to stay for about 24 hours after you woke up. They just want to check for concussion and make sure the bone is set well."

"Thanks, Grandma," Miriam said.

A few hours later, Miriam was fully awake, and a nurse was teaching her how to use crutches. She could spend a week home from school so the leg could start healing before getting bumped around. Miriam was just sitting back down on the bed when the door opened, and Sydney burst in.

"Miriam, you missed another get-together! I don't know if we can be friends anymore!" Sydney tried to keep a straight face but then walked quickly over to Miriam and hugged her tightly. Karen, Grace, Anna, and Michelle came in the door just then. They had flowers and balloons, and Anna was carrying the cake Miriam and her grandma had made.

"I called them on my way to the hospital Friday night so they would know what happened to you," Grandma said.

"We were so worried," Sydney told Miriam. "I was so relieved when she called today to say you were awake. We decided to bring the party to you."

"You guys are great!" Miriam cried. They talked and laughed and ate cake. Miriam barely felt any of her aches while her friends were there. They left after about an hour since they had to get ready for school the next day.

Miriam went home Tuesday morning. She was pushed in a wheelchair to Grandma's car, but she had to use the crutches when she got home, and it took her a while to walk from the car to the living room. Miriam was tired by the time she reached the couch. She laid down and quickly fell asleep. Grandma woke her up when it was time for her to take her pain medication. She spent her days in the living room practicing with her crutches and resting. She played piano a few times and read a lot. One or two of her friends stopped by every afternoon and delivered some of the make-up homework she would have to do. None of them brought up show choir, but Miriam didn't ask. She noticed that Angela, Krystal, and Cassidy didn't stop by or call at all. She hoped that they were just in trouble with their parents and grounded. She would find out on Monday.

Grandma would have to drive her to and from school until her cast came off and then she would have to ride the bus. Miriam asked if they could leave a little early on Monday so she could stop in and talk to the choir director, Mr. Nuskett. She also knew it would take her a while to hobble through the school. Grandma agreed.

Mr. Nuskett was unlocking the choir room door when Miriam walked up. He turned when he heard the sound of her crutches.

"Glad to see you back, Miriam."

"Thanks, Mr. Nuskett. I came by early to talk to you about show choir," Miriam told him.

"Come on in," he said as he walked through, turned on the lights, and held the door open for Miriam.

"I guess it's pretty obvious that I can't do show choir anymore," Miriam said as she entered the room. "Even after the cast is off, I'll need physical therapy and won't be able to dance around. Can I switch back to the general choir?"

"It really is too bad you can't join us for the show choir competition, Miriam. You were doing quite well," he said. "I can let you switch back to choir, but I'm not sure if you'll be able to perform with us for the school performance, as the class has been working on the pieces for a while now. You'll have to put in a lot of effort to catch up."

"I'd like to try. I will actually have more time after school, too, as I can't lifeguard with a broken leg, either," Miriam said.

"Okay. Let's see how it goes then," he replied. "Do you need help getting to your homeroom?"

"I should be fine if you could just get the door for me again."

In her homeroom, Miriam gave her teacher the doctor's note and asked to move her seat near the door so it was easier to get in and out with crutches. She would have to ask all her teachers to sit near the door throughout the day. Her friends helped her with the doors as they could. She kept her eyes out for her show choir friends but didn't see them in the hallway until after choir ended.

"Angela," Miriam called as the three girls started to walk away. Angela turned back then said something quietly to Krystal and Cassidy. Cassidy started walking back towards Miriam, but the other two walked around the corner.

"I'm so glad you three are okay," Miriam said.

"You almost killed us," Cassidy said, glaring at Miriam.

"What?" Miriam exclaimed. She wasn't expecting Cassidy to be mad at her. "I remember you pulling on my arm before we crashed."

"Oh, so you want to make it my fault? You were driving, Miriam. We trusted you to get us safely to Angela's house. All of our parents are planning to go to your court date," Cassidy said.

"I'm not blaming you, Cassidy," Miriam told her. "It was an accident. I'm dealing with a broken leg, totaled car, no job, and I probably won't drive for a very long time. Isn't that enough?"

Cassidy didn't say another word but just stormed off. Miriam couldn't keep up with her. She stopped for a minute and leaned back against a wall. She had to fight to stop her tears. Now she had lost some friends, too. After a minute, she pulled herself together and headed toward her next class. She still had some great friends, and she at least now knew who her true friends were.

The tables were turned as Steph helped Miriam go to classes and carry her books. Steph came over after school a few times a week to help Miriam catch up on the choir music. Miriam had the songs down fairly quickly — it was much easier to sing without dance moves. If she positioned herself just right, she could still play piano for about 15 minutes at a time since her leg was at an awkward angle. She mostly practiced the music for choir, as she wanted to make sure Mr. Nuskett had full confidence in her. She would get her cast off one week before the concert in mid-May, and she wanted to sing with them.

In March and April, Miriam invited her friends to have their monthly get-togethers at her house. Her grandma got over being upset with her after the first week. She saw how sorry Miriam was and believed that the accident resulted from making a bad decision. Miriam was sure the reason

Grandma had been so upset initially was that she had been afraid that Miriam would die as her daughter and son-in-law had. Miriam wasn't sure when Grandma would be ready to let her drive again. They heard in March that the court date would be at the end of May. The judge had wanted Miriam to heal first. Grandma knew someone at church who was a lawyer and would help them for free. She did warn them that Miriam could face up to five years without a license, community service time, and a fine of up to $3,000. Miriam tried not to think about it too much. It was hard to believe a judge would give her the maximum sentence for one bad mistake.

Mr. Nuskett told Miriam in early April that she could definitely join the choir for their performance. He also told her he hoped she would try the show choir again next year. She wasn't sure about that but told him thanks. Her friends were very happy for her, and Steph said she'd ask if they could stand together, just in case Miriam's leg started bothering her. That same day, he announced that the show choir placed third in the state competition. Miriam had seen some of her show choir friends in the hall, but they all ignored her. The worst day was when she dropped her science book, and Krystal was walking nearby. She actually kicked it farther away from Miriam instead of helping her pick it up. She wouldn't want to sit through show choir practices if Cassidy, Krystal, and Angela were going to act like she was invisible. General choir gave her a chance to sing and perform, but still have time for her friends and a job. *Yes,* Miriam thought, *I'm going to stick with plain old choir for high school.*

"Why won't my leg move?" Miriam asked the doctor after he took off the cast. She was telling her knee to bend, but it wasn't moving. He gently held her foot and moved her knee joint up and down.

"Give it a day or two to get used to receiving a signal from your brain again," he said. "It's been in 'lazy' mode for a while; it forgot what it's supposed to do. Mrs. Rodgers, if you come over here, I can show you how to help move her knee and foot until she can do it."

The doctor showed Grandma which exercises to do, then told them Miriam would still need to use crutches until the physical therapist could evaluate her and determine how long she would need them. She had an appointment in three days.

"Be careful the next few weeks," the doctor said as they got ready to go. "It doesn't happen often, but sometimes people re-break their bones after they get their casts off by bumping into someone or something."

"Yikes!" Miriam responded. "I definitely don't want to do that! I need to get back to lifeguarding to save up money for a new car."

The physical therapist told Miriam she would need to use the crutches for another four weeks until she could bear her full weight on her leg again. She would have to use crutches on stage for the choir performance, so Mr. Nuskett put her at the bottom row of the risers on the far right. He did let Steph stand by her in case she needed help. There were eight songs sung by the choir and three solos. After the last solo, with two songs left, the lights flickered a few times, and the power went out for a few seconds. There was just time for a few gasps, then the lights were back on. When Mr. Nuskett went to play the music to go along with the second to last song, the music system didn't work. He tried for a few minutes, then Miriam noticed his shoulders sag. He slowly walked over to the choir and spoke to them in a quiet voice.

"We're going to have to sing the last two songs a cappella, guys," he said.

Miriam looked around the room and saw the piano was still off in the wings of the stage.

"Actually, Mr. Nuskett, I can play the songs on the piano if you want," Miriam spoke up.

"Really, Miriam?"

"Yes, I've been playing them at home for practice," she replied.

"Okay. Steph, help her get set up at the piano, then come back on stage," Mr. Nuskett said. "Do you need anyone to turn pages?"

"You could ask my grandmother to come help me."

"Can you get her, too, Steph? I'll make an announcement that the show will go on," he said.

Steph helped Miriam to the piano and handed her the sheet music for the two songs. Then, she went to get Miriam's grandma.

"Ladies and Gentlemen," Mr. Nuskett announced in a very loud voice, as the microphones weren't working either. "We are having some technical difficulties. It looks like our sound system did not like the power surge just now. We are lucky to have a talented pianist in our choir, so Miriam Stanley is going to play our music for the last two songs."

Miriam heard their applause as Grandma came to stand beside her.

"So, you're saving the day on the piano again, Miri," Grandma said with a smile.

"It would look like it; I'll nod when I need the page turned if that's okay."

"Sounds like a plan," Grandma agreed.

"Are you ready?" Mr. Nuskett asked as he came to the edge of the curtain. She'd just barely be able to see him from the piano, but it should work.

"I am," Miriam replied.

"Thank you!" he said as he walked back to the middle of the stage. He lifted his hands, and Miriam began to play. Miriam sang as she played, although only Grandma could hear her voice. There was loud applause after both songs. Mr. Nuskett came to get her after the second song, and the crowd stood when she appeared. She looked back toward Steph and saw the whole choir was smiling at her, too. She felt silly bowing with Mr. Nuskett but did it anyway. She was just glad to help the choir.

There was a small reception with cookies and punch after the show, and parents kept coming up to Miriam, thanking her for playing. After about 10 minutes, she found Grandma and asked if they could go home.

"Ready to leave already?" She seemed surprised. "So many people want to thank you."

"I know, and it's sweet, but it's not like I saved the world. I just played piano," Miriam said, still smiling. "It's my leg, actually. It's feeling sore after all that standing and then the way I had to sit at the piano."

"That makes sense. I think heading out would be a good idea."

Feeling tired, Miriam said goodbye to her friends. She fell asleep in the car, and Grandma had to wake her up when they got home. She went upstairs, brushed her teeth, and fell asleep in her clothes.

The last few weeks of school went by quickly. Barely a day went by without someone asking Miriam how she got so good at playing the piano. They had a sleepover on the last day of school before most of them left for their summer trips. Miriam only had a week until her court date. Her friends wished her luck, and Steph said she'd come with Miriam since her family wasn't going to Europe until July.

Chapter 13

"Miriam Stanley, please stand," the judge said. She wore her gray hair in a low bun, and her blue eyes looked stern. Miriam stood up with her crutches for support. "We are here today to review the accident on the night of February 12th, when the vehicle you were driving hit a truck. You had three passengers in your vehicle despite your license's restriction that you have no passengers until you have had your license for one year. While damage was done to both vehicles, it is my understanding that you were the only one hurt. Is that correct?"

"Yes, ma'am. I broke my leg," Miriam replied.

"You may sit down now. My deputy is going to read the accident report, and the parents of Cassidy Swann, Angela Curtiss, and Krystal Strambach have submitted a statement that will also be read. Then, Miriam, I will give you the chance to share before I decide your punishment."

Miriam sat back down and listened carefully as the accident report was read. There was nothing surprising in the report, although she hadn't heard the statement the truck driver had made about not having any time to swerve out of the way. Then, she listened to the statements from the parents of the people who used to be her friends.

"We humbly ask the court to fully enforce the law when it comes to the case of Miriam Stanley's reckless driving on the night of February 12th," the statement began. "Her decision to take our three precious daughters into her vehicle then drive in a reckless manner almost cost five people their lives that night. Her decisions show a lack of good judgment, which is a requirement for anyone to be a safe driver. Letting her off with anything but the full punishment will show other teen drivers that safety is not the first priority in this state when it comes to driving. Thank you."

"Does it say why none of the families are here today in court?" the judge asked her deputy.

"Yes, ma'am," he replied. "It says on the attached note that they are all out of state on their summer vacations."

"Well, that speaks to their priorities," the judge said quietly, but Miriam could hear her. "Miriam, will you please stand again?"

Miriam stood up and smoothed down her shirt. She looked up and made eye contact with the judge.

"In your own words, please tell me what happened the night of the accident," the judge said.

Miriam described how her friends had asked her to take them home that night and that even though she didn't want to and knew she shouldn't, she let them convince her that it would be okay.

"I was really trying to drive safely, but Cassidy reached over and grabbed me, pulling me towards her. The steering wheel moved, and I remember trying to sit back up and straighten it out, but then we crashed.

"I realize that I made a grave mistake, and I realize why new drivers should gain experience without passengers for a few months. I am truly sorry for what happened and am very grateful I was the only one who got hurt."

"Thank you, Miriam. I can see that you are truly sorry. From the report filed by your lawyer, you have good grades, work as a lifeguard, and are active in the school choir and Kindness Club. Everyone makes some mistakes, although the one you made could have had unalterable consequences.

"You will have a suspended license for six months and will need to complete a certified driving course and do 300 hours of community service during that time. After that, you may take the driving test. If you pass, your probation will be one year with no passengers except immediate family over the age of 18. You will not be fined.

"This is a one-time warning for you, Miriam. Please take driving seriously. If anything else crops up in the next few years, this record will come up, and your punishment will be much more severe."

The judge banged down her gavel, and Miriam was dismissed. They walked out of the courtroom, and Miriam was hugged tightly by both Grandma and Steph.

"That's not too bad," Steph said.

"No, not at all!" Miriam agreed. "I think there's a lot of community service I could do at the recreation center with kids this summer and still be able to lifeguard and earn some money. That is, if Grandma will drive me."

"Of course I will, Miriam. Six months will go by quickly, and then you'll be driving again. There was a little money from insurance from your car being totaled, and this will give you time to earn some more and take the driving class."

"Very true. I'm so glad there wasn't a fine involved, too," Miriam agreed.

"Let's go get some ice cream and then talk to Mrs. Hazelton at the Rec Center about volunteering," said Grandma.

"Sounds good," Miriam and Steph said at the same time. They laughed and followed Grandma to her car. Miriam felt lighter and happier to now know what she had to do to drive again. *Thank God for second chances*, she thought.

Mrs. Hazelton was delighted to have Miriam help during the summer — for free. Miriam would help with the kids' sports camps until her physical therapist cleared her for swimming, which should only be two or three more weeks. Then, she could resume lifeguarding and volunteer to help with swim lessons. She would be able to log 20-30 service hours a week, so if all went well, she could get all 300 hours done during the summer. Steph even offered to help along with Miriam at the Rec Center a few hours a week. Grandma said they would sign her up for the driving class when school started back up.

The summer went by very fast for Miriam. Junior year would be starting in just a few weeks. Plans were in place for the final summer sleepover. Miriam and her friends started talking about college more than they ever had before. Steph was going to try to get into the University of Michigan to become a music teacher. Sydney was thinking of doing pre-med, Michelle was going to find a local school to become a teacher, while Grace was thinking of going to pharmacy school. Only Karen and Miriam couldn't pin down where they wanted to go or what they wanted to study. They knew they had a full year before they needed to start applying to colleges, but it was hard to see her friends so sure of what they wanted to do. Miriam thought if she didn't have a better idea before she visited Orphan Wish Island, she would wish to know what career path she should follow. It wasn't the most fun wish — especially for her last wish — but it would be very helpful.

Miriam and Steph joined choir again. Miriam had two classes with Krystal, but they just sat on opposite sides of the room. The "car crash girls," as her friends called Krystal, Angela, and Cassidy, didn't talk to Miriam or her friends at all. They just completely ignored them whenever they were near each other.

Miriam spent her time doing homework, practicing piano and singing, doing some lifeguard shifts, and attending driver's education classes. The driver's education instructor contacted the judge and got permission for Miriam to drive no more than 10 hours a week for the driving class with an instructor or her grandmother until the end of November, when she could retake the driver's test. She rarely thought about her wish until plans started forming for the Halloween party, which would celebrate Miriam's birthday, too, just two weeks late.

She was fairly quiet on the anniversary of her parents' deaths this year — her friends noticed and questioned her at lunch. She didn't talk about her parents much, but all her friends knew what had happened.

"Why are you so quiet today, Miri?" Sydney asked at lunch.

"Today's the anniversary of my parents' deaths," Miriam replied. "It's hitting me hard this year for some reason. It's been nine years now, and I only had them around for eight years."

Steph wrapped her arm around Miriam and gave her a hug.

"Is there anything we can do to help you?" Anna asked.

"I don't think so," Miriam replied. "I'm okay. I just want to think about them today."

"Well, we're here if you want to talk or be distracted," Karen said.

"Thanks. A distraction might be good. Let's talk about something else."

Sydney asked them if any of them had seen the new Tim Jones movie, and they all started talking about movies. Miriam remained quiet but listened to her friends chat.

That night, she pulled out her copy of Robin Hood that her parents had wanted to give her the year they died. She shed some tears and thought hard about everything she could remember about her parents. She was consoled a bit by the fact that she would be able to hear their voices again in just a few days. She'd have to think hard between now and then as to what she should wish for on the island.

On a full moon, when the lights blink three,

the door will connect to your family tree.

Only orphans may enter and find what they seek,

Open the door. Be brave, not meek.

Miriam stopped for a few moments before opening the door. There would be only one more time after this that the words would appear. She wanted to memorize how it looked. She ran her finger over each letter, then took a deep breath and opened the door.

Every time she opened the attic door to Orphan Wish Island, the ocean breeze made her breathe deeply and smile. She closed the door and saw only one other person standing by the Starfruit tree. It was Lexi. It looked like it might only be the two of them again this year. Did no one believe in the possibility of magic anymore? Did orphans not want to hear their parents' voices? Did they really want to forget them?

"Hi, Miriam," Lexi said as she got closer to the tree.

"Hi, Lexi," she replied. "How did your wish go this year?"

"It went really well. I wanted to make the varsity soccer team, and I did. Not many sophomores ever made it on the team, but I practiced every day, and I got on. How about you?"

"It didn't turn out like I planned. I wanted to make show choir — and I did — but I was ignoring my old friends for new friends. I got in a car accident and had to quit show choir, but I found out who my true friends were," Miriam replied.

"Hello, girls," said the familiar voice of Stella. "I'm glad you are both here. It ended up being only you two last year, so it can only be you two this year." Stella sighed deeply.

"As you know, this is your last wish," Stella continued. "If you come back next year, you can find out what your parents wished all along for you and hear a different message from them. I'm guessing by your dedication that you will probably both be here next year."

"I wouldn't miss it for anything," Lexi said.

"Me, neither," Miriam agreed.

"Wonderful! You two have been given a great gift to connect with your parents this way. Think carefully before you make your last wish," Stella said.

Both Lexi and Miriam started looking for the Starfruit with their names on them. Miriam found hers first, picked it, and started walking down the beach. She planned to stay for a while to think and to try to keep her parents' voices in her head. When she saw Lexi start burying her fruit, she finally took a bite and made a wish.

"I wish to know what I should do with my life," Miriam whispered. Then she closed her eyes and listened to her parents' message. She replayed it over and over in her head several times and then stood up to go bury the fruit. It wasn't until she was done burying the fruit and starting to walk back to her door that Stella came up to her.

"I know you had a rough year, and I wanted to say that I'm so glad you're okay," Stella said.

"The car accident was scary," Miriam replied, not surprised that the fairy would know what happened to her in the real world. "It was tough not being able to finish out show choir, but I finally realized who my true friends are, and that is worth more than having fun on stage."

"You're becoming very wise, Miriam," Stella told her. "I hope this year brings you lots of joy and happiness."

"Thank you," Miriam replied as they reached her door. "I'll see you next year."

"Yes, see you next year," Stella said. Miriam opened her door, looked back, waved to Stella one last time, and shut the door. She couldn't help herself, but once again, she opened the door just to see if the island would be there. It wasn't. Miriam got herself ready for bed and read for a bit before falling asleep. She barely had time to think about the topic that crossed her brain almost every night — what kind of job should she start studying for?

"Next year, we'll all be adults on our birthdays!" Sydney cried after Miriam had blown out some candles on a batch of cupcakes at their monthly get-together.

"I can't wait," Michelle said. "Everyone knows senior year is a blast, and then college is going to be the best time. I'm still trying to convince Miriam to come with me to Westerly College. Don't you think she'd make a great teacher, Steph?"

"I do," Steph agreed, "which is why she should come with me to the University of Michigan to study music."

"It's months until we have to apply anywhere, guys," Miriam reminded them. "I'll figure it out by then, but I don't really think teaching is what I want to do."

"Do you have any ideas about what you want to do?" Karen asked. "I'm still not sure, but might try out business."

"That's a good path with lots of options," Miriam replied. "I think jobs like counselor, physical therapist, or child life specialist sound interesting to me. I think I want to do something where I help people."

"What about a nurse?" Karen asked. "Isn't that what your aunt is?"

"She is, and so was my mom. I think it would be a little strange to do the same thing they both did."

"I bet your aunt would love it, though," Karen said.

"Guys, Jackson just called me and asked me to the winter dance!" Anna came bursting into the rec room. For the rest of the night, they talked about boys, movies, school, and choir. Miriam hoped it would be a while before they talked about their futures again. She just didn't have a clue what she should do.

Chapter 14

Grandma and Miriam spent Thanksgiving at the local soup kitchen that year. Grandma's church got a group together to help serve a meal, and Miriam got to dish out the mashed potatoes as the guests went through the cafeteria-style line. Miriam watched the director as he kept things moving and organized and thought about having a job like that at a women's shelter. When she told Grandma about it, she said she'd ask the director what kind of degree would be suitable for that kind of job.

The next day, Miriam had her appointment to re-take her driver's test. She was confident but really worried about making even a small mistake. Grandma had been good about driving her around, but Miriam could tell that she was ready for her to be mobile again. Miriam had enough money saved up to buy a small used car, which they would do this weekend if she passed the test.

Miriam passed the written test on the first try. She only got one question wrong, and it was about speed limits in rural areas. A woman gave her the driving test. She had cropped hair and glasses and didn't smile. She pointed toward the door with her clipboard, and Miriam walked out to her car.

"I've read your file," the woman said. "I'll be watching you closely. We're going to drive over to Bachman's Grocery, down to the Spencer Playground, then back here. Do you know how to get to those places?"

"I do," Miriam replied.

"Okay, let's go," the woman said, and they got into the car.

Miriam did everything by the book. She put her seat belt on before she turned on the vehicle. She checked her mirrors twice and put on her turn signal before moving from the curb into the parking lot. She stopped at all the stop signs for a full five seconds. She slowed down for a yield sign and a crosswalk. She regularly checked her mirrors and her speed. When they parked back at the DMV, Miriam took a deep breath.

The woman told her to park the car, turn it off and meet her inside. Her demeanor was so stoic, Miriam couldn't tell if she had passed or not.

The woman asked Miriam and Grandma to come with her to the conference room.

"Congratulations," she said and finally smiled at them. "Miriam, you have passed. I am actually very impressed with how serious you are taking driving. You are the first re-test I've had that I would willingly get in the car with again. Be just as attentive out there as you were today and you won't get into any trouble with driving again."

"Thank you, Ma'am," Miriam replied gratefully.

"You can go back out front and get your picture taken for your license. Remember, you do have a probation period — one year with no passengers except immediate family over the age of 18."

The woman opened the conference room door and took them back to the main lobby. Miriam took a number and waited about 15 minutes to get her picture taken; then, she had her new driver's license in her hands.

"Shall we get some ice cream to celebrate?" Grandma asked. Without waiting for an answer, she added, "Tomorrow, we'll go car shopping. I've done a little pre-looking for you this week while you were at school. I think you'll be excited about your options."

"Thank you, Grandma, "Miriam said. Her heart felt so full and happy. She would finally be a normal teenager again.

Miriam's car was nothing special to most people, but she loved it. Grandma had found a blue car that was right in her budget and was in very good shape. It had a lot of miles on it, but the car dealer said it had been part of the estate of an older woman who had just driven it to church and the grocery store. Her son helped her keep it in good working condition so he wouldn't have to worry about her as she drove around.

Miriam's next focus was to save up for college. Over Christmas break, she took as many lifeguarding shifts as she could. Grandma often caught a ride to the Rec Center with Miriam for her morning exercise classes. On the last Friday before the break would end, Miriam noticed Grandma wasn't as chatty as usual and thought about asking her if anything was wrong but decided to just let her be. *She would tell me if something was wrong that concerned me. Maybe she didn't sleep well last night,* Miriam thought. Miriam spent her drive thinking about the get-together at Sydney's house that night before they went back to school. She had only seen Steph over the break and was anxious to get an update on Anna and Jackson's relationship. They were spending a lot of time together the month before school got out. Anna was the only one of the group that went to the winter dance, and she was glowing when she told them all about it.

When Miriam pulled up at the Rec Center, she had barely unbuckled her seatbelt when she heard Grandma fall out of the car.

"Grandma! Are you okay?" Miriam didn't hear any response as she ran around the front of the car to her. She gently touched her cheek and said her name a few times. There was no response. Two women in running gear came over, and Miriam asked them to call an ambulance. Miriam said a prayer as she felt for a pulse and breathing. Grandma had both but was still unconscious. It felt like an eternity to Miriam, but the ambulance was there in four minutes. By that time, the Rec Center director had come out, and a small crowd had gathered.

When they loaded Grandma in the ambulance, they asked Miriam if she wanted to ride along or meet them at the hospital. They told her Grandma was pretty stable and had probably bumped her head when she fell. Miriam decided to follow the ambulance in case she needed to take them home later.

The director stopped her just before she got into her car and told her not to worry about her shifts today or this weekend.

"Keep me posted on how Mrs. Rodgers is doing, please," she asked. "I'll be praying for her."

"Thank you," Miriam said, then she headed to the hospital.

In the waiting room, Miriam tried to watch TV, but she couldn't concentrate. What would happen to her if something happened to Grandma? No, she wouldn't think about that. Grandma would be fine. Nothing serious could be wrong — she was swimming with her class just yesterday.

After almost two hours, a short nurse with a clipboard in her hands called "Miriam Stanley?" Miriam stood up and walked over to her.

"The doctor would like to talk with you. Follow me," the nurse said.

Miriam followed the nurse, expecting to go to Grandma's hospital room. The nurse led her to an office instead. A balding man in a white doctor coat was sitting at a desk looking at some papers. He didn't look up until the nurse said his name.

"Dr. Mertzer, Rodger's granddaughter is here," she told him.

"Oh, thank you, Minda," he said. "Please sit down. What is your name again?"

"It's Miriam," she replied.

"Miriam. Very pretty name. How old are you?"

"I'm 17."

"And you live with your grandmother?"

"I do. My parents died in a car accident when I was eight years old. I have an aunt and uncle, but they are missionaries in Kenya. My grandma takes care of me."

"I see," he said and finally looked up from the papers and into her eyes. "I usually wouldn't discuss an adult's condition with a minor, but until I can get in touch with your aunt and uncle, I feel you should be informed about what we think happened to your grandmother. She feels I should tell you as well.

"It was a lucky thing she came under my care today. I specialize in neurological disorders."

He paused, looking to see if she understood what he said, then continued.

"Your grandmother most likely has multiple sclerosis. I will need to conduct some more tests over the next week to be sure, but the initial results fit the profile. She said she felt weak when she opened the car door, and as she stepped out of the car, her foot didn't hold her weight, and she fell. She knocked her head on something — the door or pavement — and that knocked her out for a bit. She came to very soon after arriving at the hospital.

"She has several options for taking care of herself until the condition gets really bad, but she is in the very early stages. There is no cure right now. She will probably need your help."

Miriam was stunned. She knew a little bit about multiple sclerosis from some books she had read but had never seen it up close and personal. She tried to think of something to say but just felt overwhelmed.

"Can I see her now?" she asked.

"Yes. I'll take you to her. I know this is a lot to take in, but I will help you both as much as I can," he said.

He got up and escorted Miriam to her grandma's room. He stopped at the door and let her go in by herself. She walked over to Grandma, and they hugged for a very long time before speaking.

"Did Dr. Mertzer tell you everything? I thought he could explain it better than I could. I still have a bad headache," Grandma told her.

"He said you have multiple sclerosis and that there are a lot of options right now," Miriam replied.

"I think he may be right. I have to come back for a few tests next week, but I talked to him about some symptoms I've been noticing lately, and it all fits. I thought I was just getting older and clumsier, but the clumsiness was a sign of MS," Grandma said.

"What does it mean? Will you be okay?" Miriam asked.

"I'll be okay for a while yet, most likely. I'll have good days, with a few bad days thrown in, and over the years, the bad days will increase as my nervous system breaks down."

"Oh, Grandma, I'm worried," Miriam said.

"It'll be okay, dear," Grandma told her and gave Miriam another hug. "They'll discharge me in a few hours, and we'll go home. I'll call Susan later and see what she thinks, too, but I think you and I will be okay. We'll keep a good eye on each other like always."

"Okay, Grandma," Miriam replied, not convinced that their lives would be normal again.

"I need a favor, though, Miri. Can you please go get us some food from the cafeteria? I'm getting hungry, and it's past my lunch time," she asked.

"Of course," Miriam said. "I'll be back in a few. I love you."

"Love you, too," Grandma replied.

Miriam hovered over Grandma the entire weekend. Aunt Susan agreed to wait, not planning to come home until all the test results were back, and the diagnosis was final. Susan tried asking Grandma a lot of detailed questions, but Grandma finally suggested she call and talk to the doctor herself. Steph came by Sunday afternoon, and she and Miriam talked for a couple of hours about what might happen. Miriam asked Steph if she could call the others and tell them what had transpired. Steph told her she would do that before heading home, as Miriam didn't want to have to go over it at school — she cried a few times just talking to Steph about it.

Grandma asked her to come sit by her on the couch before bedtime.

"I see how you're worrying, Miriam, and I know it's because you care about me and love me. However, we don't have any final answers yet. Let's make this next week as normal as possible and enjoy every day. Once the tests are done, and the doctor has a diagnosis, we can go over all of our options at that point and decide what works best for you and me. Let's not worry until we know things for sure. Can you try to do that for me?" she asked and took Miriam's hand in hers.

"I can try, Grandma," Miriam answered. "It's hard to think about .... Well, you're who takes care of me. I don't know what I would do ..."

"Miriam, shhh," Grandma said. "I'm not going anywhere for a very long time. I'm still here for you."

"I wish I hadn't made my last wish yet. I'd wish for you to not have this," Miriam said.

"I don't know if that would have worked, Miribug," Grandma said. "Let's just take this a day at a time. Do that with me?"

"I will try," Miriam replied.

"That's all I ask," Grandma told her. "Now, you should get ready for bed. There's school in the morning. I love you."

"I love you, too," Miriam replied and headed upstairs. Not worrying would be easier said than done.

When the test results were in, Grandma brought Miriam along to hear the results. It had taken two full weeks, and while Miriam tried to act normally, she had still worried a lot, and the days seemed to drag by. She wanted to know what exactly was going to happen to Grandma. Aunt Susan had asked Miriam to take careful notes and send her a detailed email.

"How are you doing today, Mrs. Rodgers?" Dr. Mertzer asked after they all sat down in his office.

"I'm doing as well as I can," Grandma replied.

"How about you, Miriam? How are you doing?" he asked

"I'm okay," Miriam said, not really feeling okay.

"Well, I know you are anxious to hear the test results, so we'll start with that. As we thought, you do have multiple sclerosis. It is in the very early stages, though."

Miriam heard Grandma sigh, and put her hand on her arm. They had both been silently hoping the results would come back with something that was easy to fix.

"Your next question is probably 'What does this mean?'" he continued. "MS is a very personal condition. It affects everyone differently and over different periods of time. Some people don't show severe symptoms for 10-20 years after the first symptoms, and some progress to a wheelchair in only a year or two.

"Even though you've been thinking about this being a possibility, I know this is a lot to take in. Instead of talking on and on and having you forget half of what I say, I put together some articles and brochures that go over the major symptoms and red flags. Any time you get a new symptom, we can evaluate what treatment options are available to help reduce it."

"Is there any treatment for the early stages?" Grandma asked.

"There isn't right now, just treatments for symptoms, and right now, your only symptom is a weak step that has only happened once. If that happens again anytime soon, then we can look at starting to treat it."

"What else should I be doing?" Grandma asked.

"I want you to see me at least once a month for a quick check-up, and we can review any and all symptoms to see how you're doing. However, if anything happens that concerns you, call to get an appointment sooner."

"Can I drive? Walk for exercise? Swim?" she asked.

"You can do everything you usually do now. As symptoms appear, we'll have to evaluate what you can do. If you feel off or weak, you probably should not do those activities. You'll have to listen to your body very carefully.

"Miriam, there is something you can do for your grandmother. You need to learn about the symptoms of MS and watch her carefully when you're around. She may not notice the symptoms, and you'll have to tell her what you see. One example that most patients don't notice, but family members do, is stepping up higher than needed when walking, as if there is a stair instead of a flat floor. Can you help us by doing that?"

"Yes, I can," Miriam said. Grandma squeezed Miriam's hand and smiled at her.

"Any more questions?" the doctor asked.

Both Grandma and Miriam were quiet. It was a lot to take in.

"Okay, well, in this folder is my contact information. If you just have a quick question, call or email me, and I'll get back to you fairly quickly. I'll help you in any way that I can."

Grandma shook the doctor's hand and then they left the office. They didn't talk until they got into the car.

"I'm really glad you're here with me, Miriam," Grandma said.

"Me, too," Miriam replied.

The next day at school, Miriam told all her friends about her grandma's official diagnosis. They all asked the same questions Miriam had in her own head, and she told them what she could.

"Most likely, Grandma will be fine for a while. The symptoms may come on slowly, or they may come quickly. Everything is going to stay as normal as possible, except she's going to ask for rides when it's convenient for people, and she has an appointment with the doctor every month. I'll keep an eye on her closely, too."

"Are you worried?" Karen asked.

"Yes, I am," Miriam replied. "I think it will be something she and I will worry about every day. My aunt is going to come in a few weeks to see for herself how Grandma is doing. I think her opinion will matter a lot to both of us."

"Let us know if there's anything we can do to help," Sydney said.

"Thanks,' Miriam replied. "How about we talk about something else now?"

Her friends changed to talking about last night's episode of *Together*, and Miriam got lost in her thoughts. She was hoping her aunt would come and tell them Grandma would be okay for a long while. She knew deep down that no one could guarantee that, though.

It was early March before Aunt Susan could get a flight home that wouldn't cost a fortune. She would be able to stay for one week and then would need to go back to the orphanage. Miriam drove Grandma to the airport to pick up her aunt. When her aunt got through security, Grandma hugged her for several minutes. When they finally separated, they both had tears in their eyes. Then Aunt Susan reached for Miriam.

"I don't know how many times it helped me over the past weeks to know you were here with her, Miri," Aunt Susan said. "You're turning out to be the family's guardian angel."

"I don't know about that," Miriam replied.

"I just have one suitcase to get at the luggage carousel. It's the light blue one," Aunt Susan said as they walked toward the luggage area.

"Did you have a good flight?" Grandma asked.

"It was uneventful, and I even slept a little bit," Aunt Susan said. "The food wasn't half bad, either. Breakfast was a bagel, and there's not many ways anyone could mess that up."

They made small talk at the airport and on the entire drive home. Aunt Susan asked a lot about how Miriam was doing at school and work. Miriam could tell Aunt Susan didn't want to talk about Grandma's MS in front of Miriam just yet. Miriam caught Aunt Susan intently staring at Grandma a few times as if she could give her a personal MRI with her eyes.

Aunt Susan wasn't hungry when they got home and asked to take a quick nap instead. Grandma and Miriam ate chili in front of the TV like they did most weekends now. Grandma had found some TV trays at a garage sale, and they watched *Wheel of Fortune* and *Jeopardy* while they ate. Grandma muted the commercials, and they chatted during that time instead. Miriam enjoyed it.

Miriam was getting ready for bed when her Aunt Susan finally woke up. She thought about trying to stay up for a bit to hear what Aunt Susan and Grandma would talk about, but she had a lifeguarding shift in the morning for Saturday swim lessons. She said goodnight to her grandma and aunt and went off to bed.

The week went by quickly. Aunt Susan took Grandma to a doctor's appointment on Thursday, and that night, both Grandma and Aunt Susan were very quiet. Miriam was waiting for Aunt Susan to talk to her about the things she should look out for and how to best take care of Grandma, but she hadn't yet. Miriam decided to bring it up at dinner on Friday night since she was taking Aunt Susan to the airport on Saturday after her lifeguarding shift.

As she was going up to bed Thursday night, she overheard her aunt.

"Even he recommends the same thing I do. It would be for the best. You can't put all that pressure on her."

"No," Grandma replied sternly. "I will not spend decades of my life in a place like that. I am doing just fine right now."

"Right now ..."

Miriam didn't want to hear any more, so she hurried to the bathroom and turned on the water to brush her teeth. Did Aunt Susan want Grandma to go live in an assisted living community? What would happen to her? Grandma seemed fine to her. What was the rush?

Miriam had trouble falling asleep as she mulled over these questions. No dreams came that night.

"Okay, I'm 17, I live here, and I want to know what is going on," Miriam said as soon as they all sat down for dinner the next night. The breadsticks to go with the spaghetti and meatballs had just been passed around. Her aunt held the basket in mid-air and just stared.

"Um... well... I ..." her aunt started to say.

"Miriam, you're right. You should know what is going on," Grandma interrupted Aunt Susan. "The doctor and your aunt and uncle want me to move into an assisted living facility 'just in case' my symptoms get worse. And I don't want to."

"But the doctor said you could stay fine for years. Why would he say you should go there?" Miriam asked.

"Well, I don't know if he said it outright, but when Susan suggested it, he said it was a good idea," Grandma said.

"What would happen to me?" Miriam asked.

Grandma looked at Susan.

"Um, you could come live with us and work at the orphanage, maybe," Aunt Susan replied.

"What? It's almost my senior year!" Miriam cried. "I don't want to leave here."

"This house suits us both just fine," Grandma said and looked Miriam in the eyes. Then Miriam realized that if they left this house, she might not make it back to Orphan Wish Island to hear her parents' final message. She had to hear their message!

"Aunt Susan, we're really doing just fine. I give her rides to most places. She's good about going to the doctor and listening to him. I also read a lot about MS and know what to look for as signs she could be getting worse. I don't think it's much different than if you lived here with her."

"Except that I'm a trained nurse," her aunt said. "Fine, I see I'm not going to win right now. But, Miriam, you have to keep me posted on her all the time, please. I can come back anytime it's needed. If her symptoms get worse, you need to know that there are only two options — an assisted living facility or a visiting nurse. I understand about your senior year, and we would find a way for you to stay and graduate here if Grandma's condition did change, okay?"

"Okay," Miriam agreed. "Please include me in these conversations, though. I need to be able to tell you my side of things."

"I will, and I'm sorry," Aunt Susan said. "I still find it hard to believe you're 17. It seems that just a few months ago you were a little kid. Time has flown by, and I should treat you like the almost-adult you are."

"Well, now that that's all settled, how about some chocolate cake for dessert?" Grandma asked.

"I thought there wasn't any dessert?" Aunt Susan asked.

"There wasn't for anyone who was going to put me in an old-folks home," Grandma replied. They all laughed, and the atmosphere felt lighter in the house.

"Grandma, why did my mom and Aunt Susan decide to become nurses?"

"You don't know that story?"

"Story?" Miriam asked.

"When they were little, and we were living in our house in North Kansas City, the street was full of young children. They would all go out and play outside all day and night. One day, a few houses down, a boy fell from a tree. Your mother and Aunt Susan were there, and they must have been about 10 or 12. A mom heard the commotion from across the street and came out. She was a nurse and helped the boy until the ambulance arrived. He ended up just needing a few stitches and had a broken arm. The girls were in awe of how calm the nurse was and how she knew just what to do to help the boy. Before the nurse came out, all the kids thought the boy would die. From that day on, they talked about becoming nurses when they grew up, and then they did."

"Wow!" Miriam remarked. "That must have been scary to see. I can see why they would want to become nurses after that."

"Any reason you're asking, Miri?" Grandma asked.

"I was just wondering why they both decided to do the same thing. It's not often that siblings do the same thing in life," Miriam said. She didn't want to tell Grandma yet that she was thinking about becoming one, too.

"True, that doesn't often happen unless there is a family business," Grandma said.

Grandma was fine for the rest of the school year — or she did a good job of hiding the MS symptoms that were showing up. When Miriam was home more in the summer, she started noticing that Grandma stumbled more often. She was more tired and started skipping some of her classes at the Rec Center. Grandma also didn't want to drive herself around much anymore. Miriam knew she'd have to bring this up at the doctor's appointment in late June. Then, Miriam came downstairs from reading one afternoon and found Grandma asleep at the table and water boiling over on the stove. She turned the stove off, moved the pan, and then woke her up.

"Grandma, I think we need to see the doctor this week," Miriam said.

Grandma looked over to the stove and saw the mess. She put her head in her hands and started crying. Miriam just sat by her with a hand on her back. When she finally quieted down, Grandma asked Miriam to hand her the phone.

"I'll call him now and see when we can get in," she said.

Chapter 15

There was a new medication Grandma could try, but it could make her sleepy, so she wouldn't be able to drive or cook. However, it could slow down the other symptoms a little. Her Aunt Susan would come and stay during the summer, and they would have a nurse come by during the school year around lunchtime to check on Grandma. Miriam had offered to stay home during the summer and come home from school during lunch, but her aunt and grandma wanted her to enjoy her last summer before college and her senior year. Plus, they all knew she needed to work for money for college. She even let it slip that she had decided she was going to go to nursing school. While they were happy about that, they didn't want her to have to deal with the pressure of taking care of Grandma and school.

It was actually nice to have her aunt around during the summer. Miriam worked as a lifeguard for as many hours as the Rec Center would offer her and spent a lot of time with her friends when they were in town. She knew some of the times with her friends were the last times they'd all be doing those things together — or at least for a while. Miriam had researched a local nursing program that would start in June next year, right after school got out. She could still live with Grandma to save money if Grandma was doing okay, or if she wasn't, there were dorms where Miriam could stay.

She waited to tell her friends about the nursing program until their end-of-summer get-together. They would have it the Friday before school started, and then she had to take her aunt to the airport the next afternoon. Monday would be the start of their senior year.

Before she left to head to Sydney's house, Grandma and Aunt Susan asked her to go talk to them in Grandma's room.

"I wanted to show you something I kept that is your mother's," Grandma said. She opened up her jewelry box and pulled out a pin. "This was your mother's nursing pin. I wanted to show it to you because if you truly want to be a nurse, I think you would want her pin when your training is complete. You can hang onto it for now, though."

Grandma handed Miriam the pin, and Miriam stared at it in her palm.

"It's not just that, though," Aunt Susan said. She went to Grandma's closet and pulled out a white nurse uniform and hat. "She kept one of your mother's uniforms, too. We thought you might want it, too, for inspiration."

Miriam held the uniform to her. She didn't know what to say, but she suddenly felt a connection to her mother that she hadn't felt in a long time.

"We're not saying you can't change your mind and become something else," Grandma said. "But we know you are old enough to treasure these, no matter what you do in life."

"Thank you so much," Miriam replied.

"They'd be so proud of you, Miri," Aunt Susan told her. Miriam hoped so and hoped to find out in just a few short months.

The back-to-school party with her friends was one of the best times they'd ever had together. Anna and Steph had steady boyfriends, and Sydney dated here and there. The rest of them decided it would be better to wait until college, and were talking about going to prom together as a group of friends.

"I've finally decided where I'm going to apply for college," Miriam told her friends as they were making ice cream sundaes. "I'm going to do the nursing program at the local state campus."

"What?" Karen said. "Are you planning to start in June or September?"

"June," Miriam replied. "Wait. How do you know they offer a June start?"

"I'm going to do the same thing!" Karen announced. "My grandmother got put in a nursing home this summer, and I saw how great the nurses were helping her get settled and taking care of her. I thought that would be something worthwhile to do with my life."

"My grandma's MS is starting to get worse, and I want to be able to help her," Miriam said.

"Maybe we could share a dorm room?" Karen asked.

"Oh, definitely!" Miriam agreed.

"Hey, don't forget I'll be going there, too," Michele said. "Maybe we should look into an apartment instead."

They talked all through the night about plans for senior year and college — and backup plans. They didn't even watch any movies that night. They picked the dates for their monthly get-togethers and promised to do an end-of-school-year bash. They all knew there would be a lot of "lasts," but they didn't want to talk about that yet.

Miriam went ahead and applied to two other nursing programs that were less than three hours away in case she didn't get accepted into the local program. Karen did the same thing. Then, she spent a lot of her spare time applying for any and every scholarship she could find. Miriam had saved enough money to get through three terms but would need more to finish the program. If she did the summer terms, it would take her three years to get a Bachelor's of Science in Nursing.

For her birthday, Miriam had her friends over for dinner. They all had jobs now on the weekends, so a sleepover wasn't going to work. They had a taco bar and cake and sat around Miriam's backyard, talking until the sun went down. She was 18 and could sense adulthood coming upon her. Her parents had only been with her for eight of those years, but thanks to the island, they had been able to influence her life for the past six years as well.

Grandma went to bed early the night the door in the attic would open to Orphan Wish Island for the last time. Miriam went to her room after finishing up the dishes and tried to read until the words appeared on the door. She couldn't read more than a paragraph or two without looking up at the door. Finally, she saw the flicker of the street lamps out of the corner of her eye and quickly put her book down on the window seat. She walked over to the attic door and watched as the words started appearing and glowing on the door. She put her hand on the knob but didn't open it right away. She was going to try to savor every moment of tonight's visit to the island. She read the words on the door a few times to commit them to memory, then finally felt ready to visit the island.

As with every visit, a perfectly warm and gentle ocean breeze hit her as soon as she stepped through the door. She closed the door behind her and gazed around the island. She didn't see anyone but started walking toward the tree in the middle of the island anyway. She was halfway there when Lexi appeared to the left of the tree. Miriam waved, and Lexi waved back.

"We both made it!" Lexi cried.

"I wouldn't have missed this for anything. I can't wait to hear from my parents," Miriam replied.

"Me, too," Lexi agreed.

Stella flew up to them just then and asked if they were ready for their final message. They both nodded.

"When you are ready, you'll do like you did before and find the Starfruit with your name on it. You'll take a bite and then you'll hear a message from your parents. You may be able to talk to them, but it's different for each person. They'll tell you if it's just a message or if you can ask them one question. Once you are ready to leave, you can bury your fruit under this tree to complete the cycle. Don't leave without saying goodbye, though. I'll wait here by the tree. You are both very lucky girls to have come back every year."

Miriam and Lexi caught each other's eyes but didn't speak. They moved together to the tree and then separated as they looked for their Starfruit. Miriam found hers a few feet from where she started looking and then walked down the beach a bit before sitting down. She held the Starfruit in her hands and looked it over for a few minutes. She wanted to memorize what the fruit looked like but also wanted to think over what she would ask her parents if she got the chance. She narrowed it down to three questions — Were they proud of her? Did they think she should become a nurse? Would they always watch out for her from wherever they were? She couldn't decide, so she decided to hear what they had to say first, and then choose one if she was given that option.

She took a deep breath, closed her eyes, and took a bite of the fruit.

"Oh, Miriam, we love you so much!" Miriam heard her mother say, just like she did every night when she was alive.

"We miss you so much!" she then heard her father say.

"We are so glad you decided to come to this island year after year," her mother told her. "We recorded our main message, but at the end, you can ask us one question."

"You made your own wishes these past six years," her father said. "We also made wishes along with you to hopefully help you as you had to grow up without us.

"When you wished for the lead in the school play, we wished you courage.

"When you wished to win the STEAM Fair, we wished you would learn compassion.

"When you wished to win the talent show, we wished you would learn to love.

"When you wished for good grades, we wished you would learn the value of hard work.

"When you wished to make show choir, we wished you would learn wisdom.

"When you wished to know the path you should take, we wished you would learn responsibility."

"We see how wonderful you have become and hope our wishes were helpful to you," her mother said. "You can now ask us one question."

Miriam knew right away which question she wanted to ask them.

"Will you always be watching over me wherever you are?" she asked.

"Always, Miriam. We've been watching, and we are so proud of you. You are making good, wise choices," her dad told her.

"We can now let you go and face the world with the lessons we would have taught you if we had been with you. We love you more than anything! Be good and be kind," her mom said.

"And be smart, Miribug. Our love is always with you," her dad added. "Bye."

"Bye," Miriam said. "I love you!"

Miriam sat for a long time with her eyes closed, replaying her parents' words in her head. They wanted her to be courageous, compassionate, loving, hardworking, wise, and responsible. She had learned many lessons about all of those things during the past few years, and she would try her best to live up to the person they wanted her to be. And, they were proud of her. She smiled as she opened her eyes and stood to go bury her Starfruit. She didn't see Lexi anymore, but Stella was waiting for her.

"Lexi left a while ago," Stella told her. "I was going to give you a few more minutes and then see if you'd fallen asleep."

"I just wanted to try to remember what they said," Miriam said. "I'm glad I was able to ask them a question."

"Not many get that chance, but usually those who chose their wishes wisely are given that opportunity," Stella replied. "Let's bury your fruit."

When the fruit was buried, Stella gave Miriam a big hug and wished her well on her life's journey.

"Those we love are never far from us," Stella said. "Never forget that."

"I won't, Stella," Miriam replied. "Thank you."

Miriam walked slowly, looking around the island and enjoying the breeze as she headed toward her door. She opened it and took one last look at the tree before stepping into her room and closing the door. She knew it was the end of her visits to the island, but she had to open the door one last time to be sure. It was the attic, but there was a small, shiny Starfruit seed on the floor. Miriam picked it up, held it to her heart, and closed her eyes. She could swear she heard her parents' voices whisper together, "Our love is always with you."

Acknowledgments

Thank you so much to my husband and children for continuing to support and cheer me on during my writing journey!

Thank you to my family and friends who read my books and show me support.

About the Author

Sarah Anne Carter is a lover of books. She is an avid reader and is a book review blogger. Writing stories since she was little, Sarah is constantly thinking of ideas that could be used as a plot for a novel. She is the author of a contemporary fiction book, The Ring. She is a journalist by trade and has written numerous  newspaper articles. She has also worked in the public relations and marketing fields. She grew up as an Air Force brat and has lived in many states and countries. Currently residing in Ohio, she spends her time enjoying her family, reading, and writing. She has published two other novels — *Life After* and *The Ring*.

Want to know more? You can reach Sarah Anne at her Web site at www.sarahannecarter.com. Please take the time to leave a review of *Orphan Wish Island* on Amazon, Goodreads, or wherever you review books!

HISTRIA
BOOKS